A CURMUDGEON'S
GARDEN OF LOVE

cur·mud·geon \,kər-'məj-ən *n* [origin unknown]
1 *archaic*: a crusty, ill-tempered, churlish old man
2 *modern*: anyone who hates hypocrisy and pretense and has the temerity to say so; anyone with the habit of pointing out unpleasant facts in an engaging and humorous manner

A CURMUDGEON'S G•A•R•of•D•E•N LOVE

COMPILED AND EDITED BY
JON WINOKUR

NAL BOOKS

NEW AMERICAN LIBRARY

A DIVISION OF PENGUIN BOOKS USA INC., NEW YORK
PUBLISHED IN CANADA BY
PENGUIN BOOKS CANADA LIMITED, MARKHAM, ONTARIO

Copyright © 1989 by Jon Winokur
All rights reserved. For information address New American Library.
Published simultaneously in Canada by Penguin Books Canada Limited.
Drawings by Everett Peck.
Author photograph by Mark Wolgin.

NAL TRADEMARK REG. U.S. PAT. OFF. AND FOREIGN COUNTRIES
REGISTERED TRADEMARK—MARCA REGISTRADA
HECHO EN DRESDEN, TN, U.S.A.
SIGNET, SIGNET CLASSIC, MENTOR, ONYX, PLUME, MERIDIAN and NAL BOOKS
are published *in the United States* by New American Library,
a division of Penguin Books USA Inc.,
1633 Broadway, New York, New York 10019,
and *in Canada* by Penguin Books Canada Limited,
2801 John Street, Markham, Ontario L3R 1B4

Library of Congress Cataloging-in-Publication Data
Winokur, Jon.
A curmudgeon's garden of love / compiled and edited by Jon
Winokur.
p.   cm.
"More than 1000 outrageously irreverent quotations, anecdotes, and
interviews from an illustrious list of world-class grouches."
ISBN 0-453-00677-9
1. Quotations, English.   2. Interpersonal relations—Quotations,
maxims, etc.   3. Love—Quotations, maxims, etc.   4. American wit and
humor.   I. Title.
PN6084.I5W5   1989
081—dc20   89-8335
                                                           CIP

Designed by Barbara Huntley
First Printing, October, 1989
1   2   3   4   5   6   7   8   9
PRINTED IN THE UNITED STATES OF AMERICA

TO THE ONE WOMAN FATE CREATED JUST FOR ME.
SO FAR I'VE MANAGED TO AVOID HER.

ACKNOWLEDGMENTS

The following well-meaning persons insisted on trying to help: Peter Bell, Reid and Karen Boates, Ron Hammes, Stephen Hulburt, Nancy Lea Johnson, Roger Land, Gary Luke, Michelle Maerov, Susan Nethery, John Paine, Al Rasof, Susan Rogers, Beth Siniawsky, Jim and Nancy Steele, LuAnn Walther, and the Wolgins of Philadelphia (especially Michael A. Wolgin). Particularly meddlesome were Norrie Epstein and Elinor Winokur.

ACKNOWLEDGMENTS

CONTENTS

INTRODUCTION

The origin of *curmudgeon* is obscure, but it may come from an old Scottish word for "grumble," or from the French, *coeur méchant*—"evil heart." Curmudgeons are really quite sensitive, but they hide their tenderness behind a crust of misanthropy. They may grumble, but they are not evil of heart.

Curmudgeons are gadflies whose bitterness is a symptom rather than a disease. They're mockers and debunkers who snarl at pretense and bite at hypocrisy out of a healthy sense of outrage. Nature, having failed to equip them with a serviceable denial mechanism, has endowed them with acute perception and sly wit. They can't compromise their standards and can't manage the suspension of disbelief necessary for cheerfulness. They attack mediocrity and fraud wherever they find them, and their principal weapon is humor.

The pantheon of curmudgeonry includes Robert Benchley, Ambrose Bierce, Oscar Levant, H. L. Mencken, Dorothy Parker, Mark Twain, George Bernard Shaw, and Oscar Wilde. It was Wilde who defined a cynic as one who knows the price of everything and the value of nothing. When it comes to love, curmudgeons aren't cynics. It is precisely because they value love that they are aghast at what usually passes for it. They hate sentimentality because it trivializes sentiment; they disdain maudlinism because it devalues genuine emotion. They don't abhor romance, just its sappiness, its clichés and delusions. Curmudgeons are iconoclasts, and love's icons abound.

Curmudgeons are not incapable of love; many of them simply decline to participate. They are not freaks. It's just that they don't yearn for someone to make their lives complete.

Curmudgeons' misanthropy is a pose. They grouse about the human race, yet they're inclined to tolerate individuals; likewise, they tend to overlook love's lunacy when they're bitten. And when in love, curmudgeons don't seem to fare any better, or worse, than anyone else. That quintessential curmudgeon, H. L. Mencken, derided love and marriage until he fell in love and married; Oscar Wilde's marriage gave way to a passionate homosexual affair that led to his ruin; Bernard Shaw conducted a series of extramarital affairs exclusively by mail; Dorothy Parker was unhappily married three times, twice to the same man.

The world of love, romance, and sex is an arena in which people make fools of themselves, a fact that curmudgeons are delighted to point out. The quotations, anecdotes, and interviews herein demonstrate that delight. Most of these observations are from the world-class curmudgeons listed on page 3, but there are also contributions from uncurmudgeonly quarters (you don't have to be a curmudgeon to make a curmudgeonly statement—even the incurably sappy can have moments of clarity).

So if you're deliriously in love, if you're under the influence of the powerful drug called romantic passion, if your heart fills with joy at the prospect of spending the rest of your natural life with the same person, this book isn't for you. On the other hand, if you have difficulty with such concepts as "communication" and "intimacy" and "supportive," if your "relationships" have been less than glorious . . . read on, and, well, take heart.

J. W.
Pacific Palisades, California
January 1989

WORLD-CLASS CURMUDGEONS

EDWARD ABBEY
GOODMAN ACE
FRED ALLEN
WOODY ALLEN
KINGSLEY AMIS
MARTIN AMIS
MATTHEW ARNOLD
RUSSELL BAKER
TALLULAH BANKHEAD
JOHN BARRYMORE
ORSON BEAN
LUCIUS BEEBE
MAX BEERBOHM
ROBERT BENCHLEY
AMBROSE BIERCE
ROY BLOUNT, JR.
DANIEL J. BOORSTIN
JIMMY BRESLIN
RITA MAE BROWN
LENNY BRUCE
HEYWOOD BROUN
WILLIAM F. BUCKLEY, JR.
HERB CAEN
TRUMAN CAPOTE
AL CAPP

G. K. CHESTERTON
E. M. CIORAN
JOHN CLEESE
QUENTIN CRISP
PETER DE VRIES
HARLAN ELLISON
JOSEPH EPSTEIN
JULES FEIFFER
W. C. FIELDS
GENE FOWLER
ANATOLE FRANCE
PAUL FUSSELL
ROBERT FROST
LEWIS GRIZZARD
BEN HECHT
ALFRED HITCHCOCK
SAMUEL JOHNSON
ERICA JONG
BEN JONSON
ALICE KAHN
GEORGE S. KAUFMAN
KARL KRAUS
STEPHEN LEACOCK
FRAN LEBOWITZ
TOM LEHRER

DAVID LETTERMAN	BERTRAND RUSSELL
OSCAR LEVANT	MORT SAHL
WILLIAM LOEB	GEORGE BERNARD SHAW
HERMAN MANKIEWICZ	HARRY SHEARER
SAMUEL MARCHBANKS	DELMORE SCHWARTZ
DON MARQUIS	IAN SHOALES
GROUCHO MARX	JOHN SIMON
MARY McCARTHY	AUGUST STRINDBERG
H. L. MENCKEN	GLORIA STEINEM
HENRY MILLER	HUNTER THOMPSON
NANCY MITFORD	CALVIN TRILLIN
WILSON MIZNER	MARK TWAIN
HENRY MORGAN	GORE VIDAL
ROBERT MORLEY	NICHOLAS VON
MARTIN MULL	HOFFMAN
VLADIMIR NABOKOV	ERIC VON STROHEIM
GEORGE JEAN NATHAN	VOLTAIRE
FRIEDRICH WILHELM	EVELYN WAUGH
NIETZSCHE	CLIFTON WEBB
GEORGE ORWELL	ORSON WELLES
DOROTHY PARKER	MAE WEST
S. J. PERELMAN	OSCAR WILDE
J. B. PRIESTLEY	BILLY WILDER
ANDY ROONEY	GEORGE WILL
HOWARD ROSENBERG	EDMUND WILSON
MIKE ROYKO	ALEXANDER WOOLLCOTT
HUGHES RUDD	FRANK ZAPPA

A CURMUDGEON'S HISTORY OF LOVE
Beginning With the Expulsion From Eden and Going Downhill From There

c. THE BEGINNING Unamused by their extracurricular activities, God ejects Adam and Eve from Garden. He tells Eve, "I will greatly multiply thy sorrow and thy conception. In sorrow shalt thou bring forth children; and thy desire shall be to thy husband, and he shall rule over thee." He tells Adam, "Because thou has harkened unto the voice of thy wife, and hast eaten of the tree, of which I commanded thee, saying, Thou shalt not eat of it: cursed is the ground for thy sake; in sorrow shalt thou eat of it all the days of thy life" (Genesis 3:16–17).

c. 6,000,000 B.C. Female Homo sapiens evolve from being sexually responsive only during brief periods of estrus to continuous sexual receptivity.

c. 4,000 B.C. Egyptians invent eye makeup.

c. 3,500 B.C. First bedroom appears in Sumeria, occupied by the head of the house while wife, children, and servants sleep on floor.

c. 1,100 B.C. First known pornography depicts Ramses III in flagrante with unidentified female.

c. 1,000 B.C. Use of first wedding ring, symbolic of fetters used to physically bind the bride to her husband's dwelling.

c. 900 B.C. Upper-class Assyrians begin wearing wigs.

c. 600 B.C. Persians begin wearing tight-fitting leather clothing.

c. 550 B.C. Greek women begin wearing men's clothing.

c. 500 B.C. First marriage contract (in which six cows are exchanged for one fourteen-year-old girl).

c. 150 B.C. Macedonian slaves auctioned in Rome; males bring equivalent of $50, females $1,000.

c. 100 B.C. First wedding cake—*thrown* at bride as part of fertility ritual.

8 B.C. Ovid publishes *Ars Amatoria,* first "how-to" sex book ("If your posterior is cute, let it be seen from behind").

c. A.D. 50 Romans invent soap.

c. A.D. 100 Publication of *Kama Sutra of Vatsyayana.*

c. A.D. 200 Goths perfect nuptial abduction—capture young maidens from neighboring villages.

c. A.D. 250 Visigoths hide weapons in church altars to fend off attempts by relatives to recapture brides.

453 Attila the Hun dies from nosebleed on wedding night.

553 Procopius publishes *Anecdota,* true account of sex scandals in court of Justinian.

c. 700 Chinese invent the brassiere.

801 Charlemagne outlaws prostitution.

860 Pope Nicholas I decrees that all Roman Catholic brides-to-be receive engagement rings sufficiently expensive to work financial hardship on their intended bridegrooms.

904 Powerful Italian noblewoman Marozia turns the papacy into a "pornocracy" by having Pope John X put to death so she can install as Pope first her lover and later her illegitimate son.

1074 Roman Church excommunicates married priests.

1094 Gondolas appear in Venice.

1174 Marie, Countess of Champagne, issues proclamation: We declare that love cannot exist between two people who are married to each other. For lovers give to each other freely, under no compulsion; married people are in duty bound to give in to each other's desires.

April 25, 1227 Courtly love reaches bizarre pinnacle when knight errant Ulrich von Lichtenstein, masquerading as Venus (in white gown, braids, headdress, and pearls) rides from Venice to Vienna with entourage of squires, musicians, and maids-in-waiting, tilting with all comers and breaking 307 lances in the process, all in devotion to mysterious lady he worshiped from afar.

c. 1450 Venice city fathers order local prostitutes to bear their breasts while plying their trade.

c. 1460 First use of codpiece—ornamental pouch worn over the groin.

1495 Syphilis epidemic rages through Europe.

1503 First widespread use of pocket handkerchiefs.

1534 Unable to secure divorce from Pope, King Henry VIII of England rejects Catholicism and creates Church of England.

May 15, 1536 Indictment of Anne Boleyn cites coerced testimony that Anne had incest with her brother George and that she had been seen "alluring him with her tongue in the said George's mouth and the said George's tongue in hers."

May 19, 1536 Anne Boleyn beheaded.

1541 Publication of anti-female diatribe, *The Schoolhouse of Women,* by Edward Goysnhill.

1542 Publication of scathing reply to Goysnhill's anti-female diatribe, *The Schoolhouse of Women,* entitled *The Praise of All Women*—by Edward Goysnhill.

1552 Mary, Queen of Scots first woman golfer.

c. 1600 First use of merkin—false female pubic hair.

1622 Puritan William Gouge advises women against addressing their husbands with unseemly pet names such as "sweetheart," "dear," and "duck"; prescribes "husband" as the only proper form of address.

1675 Nell Gwynn, mistress of Charles II, accompanies him to Oxford, where her coach is attacked by angry crowd in the mistaken belief that she is Louise de Kerouaille, another of Charles's mistresses and a Roman Catholic. Instantly realizing their mistake, she leans out of window and shouts, "Pray, good people, be civil; I am the *Protestant* whore."

1700 Germany levies tax on unmarried women.

1709 Appearance of eau de cologne.

1727 First marriage advertisement (in Manchester, England, newspaper).

1763 James Boswell contracts "Signor Gonorrhoea."

1829 Indian custom of immolating widow with dead husband (*suttee*) abolished by British government.

1839 Charles Goodyear invents vulcanization process.

1862 As token of love and remorse, Dante Gabriel Rossetti buries sheaf of original manuscript poems with dear departed wife, Elizabeth Siddal.

1864 Union General Joseph Hooker supplies prostitutes to his troops.

1866 John Ruskin, age 39, falls in love with Rose La Touche, age 11, and subsequently proposes; she declines.

1869 Having reconsidered his romantic gesture, Dante Gabriel Rossetti exhumes wife, retrieves and subsequently publishes buried poems.

1903 Marie Curie first woman Nobel Prize–winner.

1904 Woman arrested in New York for smoking in public.

1906 Test for syphilis developed by August von Wasserman.

1910 Eighty-two-year-old Leo Tolstoy flees from wife, dies in railway station of exposure.

—— Mann Act bans interstate transportation of women for "immoral" purposes.

—— U.S. divorce rate 8.8 per 100 marriages.

1914 Margaret Sanger coins term "birth control."

1916 Margaret Sanger sentenced to one month in jail for starting birth-control clinic.

—— Women's International Bowling Congress founded.

—— Jeanette Rankin first woman in U.S. Congress.

1919 First widespread use of zippers on clothing.

—— Lady Astor first woman in British Parliament.

1920 U.S. divorce rate rises to 13.4 per 100 marriages.

—— Nineteenth Amendment to U.S. Constitution gives women the vote.

1921 Sunbury, Pennsylvania, requires women's skirts to be at least four inches below knee; New York State regulates skirt length, décolletage; Connecticut requires license for barbers who bob hair.

1922 Frank Harris publishes sexually explicit memoir, *My Life and Loves.*

1923 Supreme Court strikes down D.C.'s minimum wage for women and children.

—— U.S. Customs seizes Joyce's *Ulysses* on grounds of obscenity.

—— Average Parisian woman uses two pounds of face powder per year.

1924 Female federal employees barred from using maiden names.

1925 Episcopal Church eliminates the word *obey* from its marriage vows.

—— Tennessee outlaws sex education in public schools.

—— Bryn Mawr permits student smoking on campus.

—— U.S. Auto Club endorses women drivers.

1926 Hollywood legend Rudolph Valentino refuses to carry bride Jean Acker across threshold; she locks him out of honeymoon hideaway, sues for divorce.

1928 U.S. divorce rate hits 16.5 per 100 marriages, twice the 1910 rate.

—— Alexander Fleming discovers penicillin.

1930 First stewardesses hired to fly on United Airlines on rationale that with women working on the plane, male passengers would be reluctant to admit their fear of flying.

1931 Tommy Manville marries for first time.

1932 Amelia Earhart first woman to fly solo across Atlantic.

1933 Fan dancer Sally Rand packs 'em in at the Chicago World's Fair, comments, "I never made any money until I took off my pants."

—— First drive-in theater (Camden, New Jersey).

May 13, 1935 Heiress Barbara Hutton divorces husband "Prince" Alexis Mdivani and declares, "I shall never marry again."

May 14, 1935 Barbara Hutton marries Count Haugwitz-Reventlow.

1937 Edward VIII, King of England, abdicates to marry 41-year-old, twice-divorced American Wallis Warfield Simpson; calls her "the woman I love."

—— Matrimonial Causes Bill facilitates divorce in England.

—— "Platinum Blonde" Jean Harlow dies of cerebral edema.

—— Warren Beatty born.

1940 Pope Pius XII chides women for yielding to "tyranny of fashion."
—— Nylon stockings go on the market.
1942 Department stores in Detroit and Boston introduce "Slack Bars" for female defense workers.
—— Supreme Court upholds Nevada divorces.
1943 Errol Flynn tried and acquitted of statutory rape; "in like Flynn" enters language as epitome of sexual success.
—— Jane Russell's décolletage stars in Howard Hughes's *The Outlaw*.
1948 Alfred Kinsey publishes *Sexual Behavior in the Human Male*, revealing that many sexual acts previously considered "perverted" are practiced regularly by American couples.
1952 George Jorgenson undergoes sex-change operation, becomes Christine Jorgenson.
1954 Marilyn Monroe weds Joe DiMaggio.
1956 Marilyn Monroe weds Arthur Miller.
—— Brigitte Bardot a sensation in Roger Vadim's *And God Created Woman*.
1959 Postmaster General bans *Lady Chatterley's Lover*.
1960 Supreme Court lifts ban on *Lady Chatterley's Lover*.
—— Enovid, first commercial oral contraceptive, goes on market in U.S.
—— First publication of unabridged memoirs of Casanova.
—— Tommy Manville marries for eleventh and last time.
—— Norman Mailer stabs wife with kitchen knife, receives three-year suspended sentence after observation at Bellevue.
1962 Marilyn Monroe dies of barbituate poisoning.

1963 Valentina Tereshkova first woman in space.

—— British MP John Profumo resigns after disclosure of affair with "call girl" Christine Keeler.

—— Helen Gurley Brown publishes *Sex and the Single Girl*.

—— Kingsmen release "Louie, Louie"; lyrics rumored dirty.

1964 Go-go girls reign at discotheques across America.

1965 Massive power blackout hits northeastern U.S.; big increase in birthrate nine months later.

1966 Miniskirts!

—— Publication of complete works of the Marquis de Sade.

—— Frank Sinatra weds Mia Farrow.

—— Elizabeth Taylor and Richard Burton star in *Who's Afraid of Virginia Woolf?*

1967 Greek junta bans miniskirts.

—— Elvis Presley weds Priscilla Beaulieu.

—— Jayne Mansfield decapitated in auto accident.

1968 Jacqueline Kennedy marries Aristotle Onassis.

—— Richard Burton gives Elizabeth Taylor the 33-carat Krupp diamond.

1969 "Sex Fair" at Copenhagen's Sports Palace.

—— Dr. David Reuben publishes *Everything You Always Wanted to Know About Sex but Were Afraid to Ask*.

1970 McSorley's in New York admits first woman customer.

—— *Love Story* is box-office hit.

—— Mississippi permits first interracial marriage.

—— Germaine Greer publishes *The Female Eunuch*.

1972 Gloria Steinem founds *Ms.* magazine.

—— Alex Comfort publishes *The Joy of Sex*.

1973 U.S. Supreme Court legalizes abortion.

—— Billie Jean King defeats Bobby Riggs in "Battle of Sexes" tennis match.

—— Erica Jong publishes *Fear of Flying*.

1975 Male ophthalmologist Dr. Richard Raskin undergoes sex-change operation, becomes female tennis pro Renee Richards.

—— Congressman Wilbur Mills cavorts in Tidal Basin with stripper Fanne Fox ("The Argentine Firecracker"); she declares, "Even though the labels *stripper* and *congressman* are completely incongruous, there was never anything but harmony in our hearts."

1976 First females admitted to U.S. Air Force Academy.

—— Presidential candidate Jimmy Carter admits having lusted in his heart.

—— Elizabeth Ray, secretary to Congressman Wayne Hayes, reveals her sole duties consist of having sexual relations with her employer, says she's angry because he failed to invite her to his wedding.

1977 Janet Guthrie first woman to qualify at Indianapolis 500.

—— *Reader's Digest* pays $1.5 million in sex-discrimination case.

1978 John Rideout found not guilty of raping his wife.

1979 Michele Triolo sues Lee Marvin for "palimony."

—— Margaret Thatcher first female British prime minister.

—— *Kramer vs. Kramer* box-office hit.

1981 First case of AIDS diagnosed in U.S.

—— Jean Harris convicted of murder of Dr. Herman Tarnower.

—— Sandra Day O'Connor first woman on U.S. Supreme Court.

1982 4,000 Moonies in mass wedding at Madison Square Garden.

1985 Woman wins Iditarod dogsled race.

—— Rock Hudson dies of AIDS.

1986 *The New York Times* will use the word *Ms.* for women who specifically request it.

1987 "Date rape" growing problem on U.S. college campuses.

—— Reverend Jim Bakker admits to sexual liaison with church secretary Jessica Hahn, denies he's homosexual, resigns as head of PTL.

—— Gary Hart withdraws from presidential race after cruise on yacht *Monkey Business* with Donna Rice.

—— Miniskirts fail to make comeback; Bette Davis declares: "In my day hot pants were something we had, not wore."

—— Liberace dies of AIDS.

—— Porn Queen Cicciolina elected to Italian Parliament.

—— *Fatal Attraction* box-office hit.

1988 Andrew Wyeth's *Helga* tour begins, hyped by rumors of artist's affair with model.

—— Reverend Jimmy Swaggart admits having had sex with prostitute, expresses confidence that God will forgive him.

—— Jessica Hahn has breasts "augmented," appears nude in *Playboy*.

—— Composer of "Louie, Louie" claims lyrics aren't dirty.

↜ PAUL FUSSELL ↝

JW: *What's the difference between love and sex?*
PF: I've never understood the relation, exactly. I think you can have love without sex and obviously you can have sex without love—a great deal of that goes on. When they coincide maybe you've really got something, but I think it's fairly rare.

Let's talk about sex, because nobody knows anything about love, in my view. It's quite irrational, and as I say, you can have love without having sex. I've fallen in love with a lot of people, a lot of things, objects—even *animals*, in a way that I would define as "love" without any sexual impulse whatever. I just want to admire those people or those things and be near them all the time. And that's very different from sex, which involves the instinct of possession: You want to *have* it, you want to *get* it, you want to be *involved* in it, you want to command it.

JW: *How do curmudgeons fare, generally?*

PF: Most curmudgeons ultimately are stricken by love, no matter how skeptical they are about it. My example is H. L. Mencken, who spent most of his life sneering and ridiculing the whole idea of love, and then, when he was in his fifties, as a longtime bachelor of the old type, suddenly fell in love and got married. Shakespeare's Benedick is the classic example of this, and it's a very amusing thing, but it does make the point that even curmudgeons are not proof against the irrationalities, the charms of love. Charm is a good word because it implies something mystical, something magical, and something ultimately unfathomable.

JW: *Are Americans any less adept at fathoming this mystery than other nationalities?*

PF: No, I think everybody is equally puzzled by it. If you're talking about *sex,* I think Americans are worse at it than almost everybody else. I don't know why, but they seem to be extremely clumsy and egotistical and they have all sorts of problems that other people don't seem to have. It's partly the result of being overcivilized in certain ways. Engineering and self-consciousness, the whole current body cult, make a sex life extremely difficult today in the sense that everybody is overweight or that your *technique* is somehow faulty. I think Americans are more hung up on such questions, which have to do with sex rather than love, than most Europeans.

JW: *Do the French deserve their reputation as lovers?*

PF: I think so, probably because they don't take it seriously. It's a big, cynical game with them, like almost everything else, including literature and philosophy and warfare. It was the French who had the good sense to get out of Vietnam, leaving it to the moron Americans. They're pretty shrewd people and I think their love lives or their sex lives reflects that shrewdness. *We're* the people who take it terribly seriously and therefore get into all kinds of trouble.

JW: *What about the war between men and women?*

PF: It's flourishing.

JW: *But what are some of the essential differences between men and women? For example, is it true that women don't gamble as much as men do?*

PF: Yes, I think that's true. It was George Orwell who noted that a real thinker ultimately arrives at the conclusion that women are not stamp collectors. That means something, I don't know what, but it's obviously true. It means the same thing as the point that women are not gamblers. Women can be perfectly good symphony conductors and chess players, but I can't imagine a woman being a gambler in the way that a man is: obsessed, sitting up all night at a poker table.

JW: *Do you agree with the observation that marriage and passion are irreconcilable?*
PF: I'm not sure, but for the sake of my relatives both past and present, I'd better not comment on that.
JW: *How do you feel about "relationship" books like* Women Who Love Too Much?
PF: I don't know these books. I haven't read any of them. The minute I see a rack of them in a bookshop I leap back about ten feet, the way I do with romances and other such material. I think that to attempt to learn how to do anything out of a book, except maybe how to plane a plank or wash dishes or build a house, is misguided. You don't learn things that are really worth learning out of a book. You learn them by keeping your eyes open and watching real people and real life. You learn from your own terrible experiences.

PAUL FUSSELL is the Donald T. Regan Professor of English at the University of Pennsylvania and the author of *The Boy Scout Handbook and Other Observations, The Norton Book of Travel,* and *Thank God for the Atom Bomb and Other Essays.*

❧ ALIMONY ❧

The ransom that the happy pay to the devil.
H. L. MENCKEN

The curse of the writing classes. NORMAN MAILER

The high cost of leaving.   ANONYMOUS

Bounty after the mutiny.   MAX KAUFMANN

Billing minus cooing.   MARY DORSEY

Disinterest, compounded annually.
WALTER MCDONALD

Old wives don't die if they're getting alimony.
DAVID BROWN

A lot of women are getting alimony who don't
earn it.   DON HEROLD

Even hooligans marry, though they know that
marriage is but for a little while. It is alimony that
is forever.   QUENTIN CRISP

No one is going to take Women's Liberation seriously until women recognize that they will not be
thought of as equals in the secret privacy of men's
most private mental parts until they eschew alimony.
NORMAN MAILER

She cried—and the judge wiped her tears with my
checkbook.   TOMMY MANVILLE

Being a bachelor is the first requisite of the man
who wishes to form an ideal home.

BEVERLY NICHOLS

The only good husbands stay bachelors: they're
too considerate to get married.

FINLEY PETER DUNNE

Though he eventually married Kitty Carlyle, Moss Hart was a confirmed
bachelor when he arrived at a party with a young actress named Edith
Atwater. "Ah," said Oscar Levant, "here comes Moss Hart and the
future Miss Atwater."

A bachelor's life is a fine breakfast, a flat lunch,
and a miserable dinner.　　　　LA BRUYÉRE

Bachelors have consciences, married men have
wives.　　　　H. L. MENCKEN

A bachelor's virtue depends upon his alertness; a
married man's depends upon his wife's.

H. L. MENCKEN

A bachelor never quite gets over the idea that he is
a thing of beauty and a boy forever.

HELEN ROWLAND

By persistently remaining single, a man converts
himself into a permanent public temptation. Men
should be more careful; this very celibacy leads
weaker vessels astray.　　　　OSCAR WILDE

HENRY LOUIS MENCKEN, reporter, essayist, lexicographer, editor, was one of the most influential and prolific American social critics of the first half of the twentieth century, reaching the peak of his influence and popularity in the twenties. He unflinchingly battled the fundamentalism and Puritanism of his day, and he was the scourge of the American middle class, which he labeled the "booboisie."

Though Mencken portrayed himself as a mysogynist, he liked women. He was no stranger to chorus girls, and he was acquainted with many prominent women of his day, among them Anita Loos, Lillian Gish, and Aileen Pringle. He read love poems, and would gallantly kiss the hand of a lady when introduced. Still, he was America's most unrepentant bachelor. That is, until he astonished his friends and readers by marrying a young college instructor named Sara Powell Haardt.

They met at Mencken's annual lecture at Goucher College (entitled "How to Catch a Husband," it was actually a speech on writing). At twenty-four—eighteen years his junior—she was the youngest member of the English faculty, a frail, self-absorbed native of Montgomery, Alabama, who was active on behalf of women's suffrage. They had much in common: Both were writers, both were of German ancestry; they had many Baltimore friends in common; and they shared the same social and political views (a combination of libertarianism and a Victorian sense of propriety). They both hated sports and flowers, were both basically unemotional, and both distrusted marriage.

Their courtship lasted seven years, during which his letters to her betray an uncharacteristic tenderness: He admires her courage and cheerfulness in the face of the tuberculosis and its complications, consoles her about frequent hospitalizations, recommends specialists, and repeatedly offers to lend her money to pay the doctor bills. One hospitalization elicited what must be the closest to a whine that Mencken was capable of: "Tell [the doctor] he is not to hurt you. I can't bear to see you in pain. It must be stopped."

He was, in short, her mentor. He gave her advice and encouragement in her efforts as a writer, helped her get a contract with Paramount as a screenwriter, steered her free-lance essays and short stories to the appropriate publications, and occasionally used his influence with editors on her behalf.

When they married in 1930, the headlines blared:

MIGHTY MENCKEN FALLS
MENCKEN, ARCH CYNIC, CAPITULATES TO CUPID
WEDLOCK SCOFFLAW TO MARRY
ET TU, H. L.?

The marriage shattered his image and may even have contributed to his decline in popularity. His explanation to his confused and outraged fans was vintage Mencken: "I formerly was not as wise as I am now."

It was an idyllic marriage. He mailed her postcards with the stamp intentionally upside down, a signal that he loved her; and many of his letters ended with "I kiss your hand." He was devoted, affectionate, attentive. The Antichrist of Baltimore, the hard-bitten, cynical debunker of emotionalism, was a model husband.

With the arrival of the Depression and the election of Franklin Delano Roosevelt, Mencken's popularity began to wane and he withdrew into the marriage. They spent most of their time at home, together, working on their respective writing. He spent less and less time at *The American Mercury* and finally resigned as its editor in 1933.

The Menckens lived happily together for five years as Sara's fragile health worsened. When she died in May 1935, he mourned her loss deeply yet was able to say to a friend, "When I married Sara the doctors said she would not live more than three years. Actually she lived five, so I had two more years of happiness than I had any right to expect." And he later remarked, "I was fifty-five years old before I envied anyone, and then it was not so much for what others had as for what I had lost."

ꙅ *Mencken on Marriage* ꙅ

Marriage is a wonderful institution. But who would
want to live in an institution?

The only really happy folk are married women and
single men.

One of the aims of connubial bliss is to punish
both parties.

The fundamental trouble with marriage is that it
shakes a man's confidence in himself, and so greatly
diminishes his general competence and effective-
ness. His habit of mind becomes that of a com-
mander who has lost a decisive and calamitous
battle. He never quite trusts himself thereafter.

[Marriage is] far and away the most sanitary and
least harmful of all the impossible forms of the
man-woman relationship, though I would sooner
jump off the Brooklyn Bridge than be married.

If I ever marry, it will be on a sudden impulse—as
a man shoots himself.

Marrying is like enlisting in a war or being sentenced to a form of penal servitude that makes the average American husband into a slave.

That I have escaped [marriage] . . . is not my fault, nor is it to my credit; it is due to a mere act of God. I am no more responsible for it than I am for my remarkable talent as a pianist, my linguistic skills, or my dark, romantic, somewhat voluptuous beauty.

A man may be a fool and not know it—but not if he is married.

In marriage, for a man, in order to get the precise thing or things that he wants, he has to take a lot of other things that he does not want.

Husbands never become good; they merely become proficient.

No married man is genuinely happy if he has to drink worse whiskey than he used to drink when he was single.

A woman usually respects her father, but her view of her husband is mingled with contempt, for she is of course privy to the transparent devices by which she snared him.

The way to hold a husband is to keep him a little jealous; the way to lose him is to keep him a little more jealous.

Whenever a husband and wife begin to discuss their marriage, they are giving evidence at an inquest.

Bachelors know more about women than married men. If they didn't, they'd be married too.

No unmarried woman can be polite to a bachelor without beginning to speculate how he would look in a wedding coat. This fact, which is too obvious to need proof, makes friendly dealings with them somewhat strained.

Being married with all your friends around you is as private and as discriminating as eating in the window of a restaurant.

Getting married, like getting hanged, is a great deal less dreadful than it has been made out.

If I had to live my life over again, I don't think I'd change it in any particular of the slightest consequence. I'd choose the same parents, the same birthplace . . . the same wife.

It is a grand experience to be able to look a hotel detective in the eye.

ᚠ LOVE LETTERS ᚠ

The letter killeth.   2 CORINTHIANS 3:6

Darling Laura, sweet whiskers, do try to write me better letters. Your last, dated 19 December received today, so eagerly expected, was a bitter disappointment. Do realize that a letter need not be a bald chronicle of events; I know you lead a dull life now, my heart bleeds for it, though I believe you could make it more interesting if you had the will. But that is no reason to make your letters as dull as your life. I simply am not interested in Bridget's children. Do grasp that.
> EVELYN WAUGH to his wife

> I hope you are well and adore me as much as ever. If you want to come out [to California] I'll pay your fare as far west as Schenectady—they're not going to get me under the Mann Act.
> GROUCHO MARX to Betty Forsling

On my return . . . I find your letter, which gives me the utmost possible annoyance. Ought not your lamentations ever cease, Madame? You make me repent my frankness. . . . If you wish our relation to continue, conduct it on a less tragic note.
> HORACE WALPOLE to Madame du Deffand

> Be so good as to tell me . . . who is against my having any shirts. You can deny clean linen to the inmates of a hospital; but I do not intend to go

without it. How your meanness, that of your origin and that of your parents, shines forth in your every act! My dove, the day I so far forgot what I was that I could be willing to sell you what I am, it may have been to get you under the covers—but it wasn't to go uncovered.

MARQUIS DE SADE to his wife

Please bring my flute.

PERCY BYSSHE SHELLEY to his wife, informing her that he had eloped with Mary Godwin and asking her to join them

I have a wicked tongue, a deadly pen and a cold heart . . . I shall be angry with myself tomorrow for sending you this . . . Is it not outrageous? Burn it. Do not read it. Alas, it is too late. You *have* read it.

GEORGE BERNARD SHAW to Alice Lockett

I hope you have lost your good looks for while they last any fool can adore you, and the adoration of fools is bad for the soul. No, give me a ruined complexion and a lost figure and sixteen chins on a farmyard of crow's feet and an obvious wig. Then you shall see me come out strong.

GEORGE BERNARD SHAW to Mrs. Patrick Campbell

By this mail I am sending you a box of cigarettes. It is *not* a Christmas present. I abhor and abominate all the Christian holidays, including even Good Friday.   H. L. MENCKEN to Sara Haardt

Last night the thermometer dropped from 95 to
59. I dreamed that you and I were cruising the
Mediterranean on my 30,000-ton yacht, the *Kai-
ser Wilhelm II*, with an orchestra of 118 pieces
to entertain us, and 1,000 kegs of beer in the
hold. Today I mixed and laid concrete for
four hours.   H. L. MENCKEN to Sara Haardt

Charles Dickens sent an expensive gift to his mistress, Ellen Ternan, but
by mistake gave the messenger his home address, so Mrs. Dickens
received the package and read the enclosed love letter. The marriage
eventually disintegrated, but not before Dickens had burned all the
letters he had received during the previous twenty years.

I will marry you so gladly with the old marriage
service: for better or worse in sickness and in
health, and forsaking all others—until death do us
part. Ha!—Ha!   DOROTHY THOMPSON to her
intended, Sinclair Lewis

Dear United States Army: My husband asked me
to write a recommend that he supports his family.
He cannot read, so don't tell him. Just take him.
He ain't no good to me. He ain't done nothing
but raise hell and drink lemon essence since I
married him eight years ago, and I got to feed

seven kids of his. Maybe you can get him to carry a gun. He's good on squirrels and eating. Take him and welcome. I need the grub and his bed for the kids. Don't tell him this, but just take him.

ANONYMOUS hand-delivered in 1943
by an Arkansas man to his draft board

I am so anxious for you not to *abdicate* and I think the fact that you do is going to put me in the wrong light to the entire world because they will say that I could have prevented it.

WALLIS WARFIELD SIMPSON to Edward VIII

Loving you is like loving a red hot poker which is a worse bedfellow than even Lytton's Umbrella; every caress brings on agony.

BERTRAND RUSSELL to Ottoline Morrell

. . . My life was better before I knew you.

EDITH WHARTON to Morton Fullerton

I could not love thee, dear, so much if I did not love my freedom more.

JOHANNES BRAHMS to Agatha von Siebold,
breaking their engagement

You must make a serious effort to change, my dear Clara. . . . Passions are not a natural adjunct to human nature, they are always exceptional or aberrant . . . Look on yourself as ill, dear Clara, seriously ill . . .

JOHANNES BRAHMS to Clara Schumann

If we love we must not live as other men and women do—I cannot brook the wolfsbane of fashion and foppery and tattle. You must be mine to die upon the rack if I want you . . . Good bye! I kiss you—O the torments!

JOHN KEATS to Fanny Brawne

If it is not mere rhetoric and you really mean what you say when you say, "I will do anything you want me to do!", then let us have a real though minor trial: will you learn shorthand as soon as possible? It is a skill worth having anyway.

DELMORE SCHWARTZ to Elizabeth Pollet

It is impossible for me to continue any longer a correspondence that is becoming epileptic.

GUSTAVE FLAUBERT to Louise Colet

Almost everything you have asked for—with the exception of a mink coat—I have given you. But you show no appreciation—only boredom, discontent. You can't bear to remain at home of an evening. If you do it is only to cut your toe nails . . .   HENRY MILLER to his fifth wife

I will not meet you at the pier, as it will probably be chilly.   ANTON CHEKHOV to Olga Knipper

✌ LEWIS GRIZZARD ✌

JW: *Are Americans good lovers?*
LG: I haven't had sex with enough Americans to generalize. You'd have to have sex with somebody from every state, and the last time I checked, I've missed North and South Dakota, Maine

and Alaska. I did screw an Eskimo once, but she wasn't an American citizen. Ever try to make love in a kayak? Did you know that *kayak* spelled backwards is *kayak*? Did you know that *DUI* spelled backwards is *IUD*? Think about these things, Jon.

JW: *What's the main difference between men and women?*

LG: Women have absolutely no idea, no *comprehension*, of the infield fly rule. The infield fly rule is one of the reasons that the planet keeps turning. If you didn't have the infield fly rule and you hit a pop-up, the runners on first and second wouldn't know whether to run or not, and the infielder could screw around and not catch it on purpose . . . it would be chaos! When I try to explain the infield fly rule to women, they look up at me and say, "The what?"

JW: *You've been married several times . . .*

LG: Three. And I just got engaged the other day. Bought her a ring that cost six hundred dollars.

JW: *What's your advice to men about to embark on the sea of matrimony?*

LG: If you don't have control of the TV remote, you ain't nothin'! Two of my divorces were a result of the struggle to see who was going to control the TV remote. I've written a prenuptial agreement: I get the clicker! If we get divorced, she gets the house, all my cars, all my dogs . . . I get the clicker and the small television.

JW: *How do you get along with your ex-wives?*

LG: I have one in Montana, one in Chicago, and one in Charlotte, so our paths don't cross very often. I'm not on bad terms with any of them—I've just told them that if they come near my house I'll kill 'em.

JW: *What's the difference between sex in the South and sex in the North?*

LG: You don't have to screw as many girls with hairy legs in the South.

JW: *What's the difference between love and sex?*

LG: Sex is a lot messier than love. There's nothing inherently dirty about sex, but if you try real hard and use your imagination you can overcome that.

JW: *Do you read "relationship" books?*

LG: No, I don't even use the word *relationship*. Unless you're screwin' your cousin; that's a "relationship."

JW: *Have you ever read Shere Hite?*

No. I only read history and pornography.

JW: *Do you watch X-rated movies?*

LG: Yes, I went to see one the other night called *Jilly Goes to the Dentist for a Fillin' and a Drillin'*, and frankly I enjoyed it a lot more than I did *Heartburn,* with Jack Nicholson and Meryl Streep, for a couple of reasons. One, Meryl Streep is a dog. She's a good actress, but the girl is a dog. She reminds me a lot of Cordie Mae Poovey, a girl I went to high school with. She played a great trumpet, but god*damn* she was ugly.

JW: *Describe your ideal woman.*

LG: Deaf and dumb; her father owns a liquor store; she's a graduate of the University of Georgia; gives me absolutely no crap about anything on this earth; cooks marvelous pork chops and country-fried steak; loves the Lord; gives me back massages; doesn't whine; doesn't say things like, "I'm cold, when is this gonna be over?" when you take her to the ballgame.

JW: *What do you think of feminism?*

LG: You mean all them wild women at the National Organization for Women? All them women who scream and raise hell and don't like anything? I think if a woman can do the same job as a man, she should have equal pay. I just don't think women should be allowed to drive or play golf. If I could only pick one, I'd get them off the golf course.

JW: *What's wrong with women on the golf course?*

LG: The average woman can't hit the son of a bitch out of her shadow. Now, I'm a high handicapper, but when I get to six, I put that sucker in my pocket and go on to the next hole. Women will keep hittin' it, even if it takes thirty-seven shots. At my club we don't allow women on the golf course. One got on the other day and we shot her.

JW: *Have you ever tried phone sex?*

LG: Phone sex? When you call up somebody and say, "Wanna have some sex?

JW: *No, where you call a 976 number and hear an obscene recording.*

LG: I didn't know about that. Tell me more! I'll call tomorrow!

JW: *Are the rich different when it comes to love or sex?*

LG: They get to have sex in nicer places. The sheets are cleaner. While we're screwin' around with some hussy in a Motel 6, the rich have somebody up in a suite in the Ritz Carlton. While we're drinkin' Budweiser, they're drinking Dom Perignon.

JW: *What's the role of men's mothers in the war between men and women?*
LG: We have no chance against women. We've never had a chance. There's no way we can win. But as long as we've got momma, at least we've got *somebody* on our side. I think most of us go out and try to find our mothers, but I've yet to find a woman who will give me a tub bath.
JW: *In spite of your attitude, isn't it true that most of your readers are women?*
LG: Right. See, they all think they want Phil Donahue . . . till they get 'im. Then they want somebody like Raunch Botts. I had a woman tell me that all those guys like Phil Donahue are a bunch of wimps and that women really like sons of bitches. She told me that she knew a guy who always sent her flowers, took her to the finest restaurants, took her *antiquing*. She said he was the dullest son of a bitch that ever was. The guy she really loved never called her, ran around on her, got drunk and stood her up. She loved 'im.
JW: *Raunch Botts?*
LG: Raunch Botts. He's a bad person who don't wash his feet and don't love the Lord, but's he's a sexy guy. He was Lounge Lizard of the Year in 1974. Women love 'im.
JW: *Aside from Raunch Botts, what do women want?*
LG: I once heard a comedian say that what women really want is your dick. They want to put it away somewhere, and when you go out, they want you to have to beg: "Sweetie, some of the guys are goin' to the game tonight; can I take my dick?" "Of course you

can't take it!" "Well, all the other guys are takin' theirs. . . ."
That's what they want, they want your balls in their pocket.
They're basically bad people. But I love 'em.

LEWIS GRIZZARD is a nationally syndicated columnist. His most
recent book is *Don't Bend Over in the Garden, Granny, You Know
Them 'Taters Got Eyes*.

❧ DIVORCE ❧

Fission after fusion.   RITA MAE BROWN

Divorce dates from just about the same time as marriage; I think that marriage is a few weeks the more ancient.   VOLTAIRE

Divorces are made in heaven.   OSCAR WILDE

You never really know a man until you have divorced him.   ZSA ZSA GABOR

Zsa Zsa Gabor is an expert housekeeper. Every time she gets divorced, she keeps the house.
     HENNY YOUNGMAN

Getting divorced just because you don't love a man is almost as silly as getting married just because you do.   ZSA ZSA GABOR

Paper napkins never return from a laundry, nor love from a trip to the law courts.
     JOHN BARRYMORE

Why do Jewish divorces cost so much? Because they're worth it.   HENNY YOUNGMAN

For a while we pondered whether to take a vacation or get a divorce. We decided that a trip to Bermuda is over in two weeks, but a divorce is something you always have.   WOODY ALLEN

Remarriage is an excellent test of just how amicable your divorce was. MARGO KAUFMAN

The only solid and lasting peace between a man and his wife is, doubtless, a separation.
LORD CHESTERFIELD

❖━━━━━━━━━━━━━━━━━━━━━━━━━━━━━━❖

Norman Mailer passed away yesterday after celebrating his 15th divorce and 16th wedding. When asked on one occasion why he married so often, the Pulitzer Prize-winner replied, "To get divorced. You don't know anything about a woman until you meet her in court."
NORMAN MAILER's mock obituary for himself

❖━━━━━━━━━━━━━━━━━━━━━━━━━━━━━━❖

The difference between divorce and legal separation is that a legal separation gives a husband time to hide his money. JOHNNY CARSON

The happiest time of anyone's life is just after the first divorce. JOHN KENNETH GALBRAITH

When a couple decide to divorce, they should inform both sets of parents before having a party and telling all their friends. This is not only courteous but practical. Parents may be very willing to pitch in with comments, criticism and malicious gossip of their own to help the divorce along.
P. J. O'ROURKE

Being divorced is like being hit by a Mack truck.
If you live through it, you start looking very carefully to the right and to the left.   JEAN KERR

> In our family we don't divorce our men—we bury
> them.   RUTH GORDON

Whenever I date a guy, I think, is this the man I
want my children to spend their weekends with?
                                           RITA RUDNER

ʕ FEMINISM ʔ

In the world we live in, feminism is a trivial cause.
DORIS LESSING

The woman's movement is no longer a cause but a symptom. JOAN DIDION

This is what sexual liberation chiefly accomplishes—it liberates young women to pursue married men.
GEORGE GILDER

Nothing would induce me to vote for giving women the franchise. I am not going to be henpecked into a question of such importance.
WINSTON CHURCHILL

Women's liberation is just a lot of foolishness. It's men who are discriminated against. They can't bear children. And no one's likely to do anything about that. GOLDA MEIR

People call me a feminist whenever I express sentiments that differentiate me from a doormat or a prostitute. REBECCA WEST

Whatever women do they must do twice as well as men to be thought half as good. Luckily this is not difficult.
CHARLOTTE WHITTON on becoming mayor of Ottawa

I would rather lie on a sofa than sweep beneath it.
SHIRLEY CONRAN

In the eighteenth century, when logic and science
were the fashion, women tried to talk like men.
The twentieth century has reversed the process.

ALDOUS HUXLEY

Beware of the man who praises women's liberation; he is about to quit his job. ERICA JONG

No man is as anti-feminist as a really feminine
woman. FRANK O'CONNOR

The major concrete achievement of the women's
movement of the 1970s was the Dutch treat.

NORA EPHRON

I'm furious about the Women's Liberationists. They
keep getting up on soapboxes and proclaiming
that women are brighter than men. That's true,
but it should be kept very quiet or it ruins the
whole racket. ANITA LOOS

Boys don't make passes at female smartasses.

LETTY COTTIN POGREBIN

How much fame, money, and power does a woman
have to achieve on her own before you can punch
her in the face? P. J. O'ROURKE

Women are equal because they are not different
any more. ERICH FROMM

We will have equality when a female schlemiel moves ahead as fast as a male schlemiel.

> ESTELLE RAMEY

> I can't think of anything more aggressive than actually sticking something into someone.
>> GRAHAM HILL on why men are better drivers than women

They have a right to work wherever they want—as long as they have dinner ready when you get home. JOHN WAYNE

> Women are not men's equals in anything except responsibility. We are not their inferiors, either, or even their superiors. We are quite simply different races. PHYLLIS McGINLEY

Scratch most feminists and underneath there is a woman who longs to be a sex object. The difference is that is not *all* she longs to be.

> BETTY ROLLIN

> It is naive in the extreme for women to expect to be regarded as equals by men . . . so long as they persist in a subhuman (i.e., animal-like) behavior during sexual intercourse. I'm referring . . . to the outlandish PANTING, GASPING, MOANING, SOBBING, WRITHING, SCRATCHING, BITING, SCREAMING conniptions, and the seemingly invariable "OH MY GOD . . . OH MY GOD . . . OH MY GOD" all so predictably integral to pre-, post-, and orgasmic stages of intercourse. TERRY SOUTHERN

When a woman becomes a scholar there is usually
something wrong with her sex organs.

NIETZSCHE

Despite a lifetime of service to the cause of sexual
liberation, I have never caught venereal disease,
which makes me feel rather like an Arctic explorer
who has never had frostbite.

GERMAINE GREER

The women's liberation warriors think they have
something new, but it's just their armies coming
out of the guerrilla hills. Sweet women ambushed
men always: at their cradles, in the kitchen, the
bedroom . . .   MARIO PUZO

Many books today suggest that the mass of women
lead lives of noisy desperation.

PETER S. PRESCOTT

I'm the most liberated woman in the world. Any
woman can be liberated if she wants to be. First,
she has to convince her husband.

MARTHA MITCHELL

When a woman behaves like a man, why can't she
behave like a nice man?   DAME EDITH EVANS

The ironic side effect of women having abandoned
their privileged status as "ladies" is that they are
now in danger of being as revolting as men, and
accordingly treated, by men, as nothing special.

QUENTIN CRISP

Women now have the right to plant rolled-up dollar bills in the jockstraps of steroid-sodden male strippers. HOWARD OGDEN

What's the point of being a lesbian if a woman is going to look and act like an imitation man? RITA MAE BROWN

Women are the only exploited group in history to have been idealized into powerlessness. ERICA JONG

Some of us are becoming the men we wanted to marry. GLORIA STEINEM

A woman who strives to be like a man lacks ambition. ANONYMOUS

No one should have to dance backward all their lives. JILL RUCKELSHAUS

JW: *You've been married five times . . .*
HE: Here is my message to everybody out there: If I, after four wretched marriages and a whole lifetime of fucking up people's

lives, and having them fuck up my life, could arrive at a marriage as happy and terrific as I've got, *anybody* can do it. Jack the Ripper could do it. Heinrich Himmler could do it. Unlikely as it seems, even human offal like Geraldo Rivera and Morton Downey, Jr., could do it. We're talking here about a man with a face of a dog and a woman with the body of a centipede—*they* could be happy! If *I* can be happy, anybody in this universe can be happy.

JW: *What went wrong in the past?*

HE: The problem was a combination of dopey circumstances and cornball attitudes; but basically I was brought up as a nice middle-class Jewish boy in the thirties and forties in Ohio and I went for the okey-doke: I believed that old ramadoola about marriage, 2.6 children, and a station wagon in the garage, because that was the banner America flew all those years. Well, I married fairly young the first time, utterly innocent—well, not so much innocent as *dopey*. I was world-class dopey. I ran away from home when I was thirteen, so I knew virtually nothing about women. I never kissed a girl until I was eighteen years old, and I don't think I got laid until I was nineteen or twenty. And I was married at twenty-one. I stumbled through my own life—as most people do—like someone stunned by a ball-peen hammer. I had no more idea of what I was about than any teenager today. The difference, I suppose, is that they have much more familiarity with sex. The average age of defloration for young women in this country is twelve or thirteen. When I was a teenager it was twenty-one or twenty-two. Big difference in available years to mature.

We really didn't know anything and we *knew* we didn't know

anything. The whole idea of going to buy a condom—it was that old Lenny Bruce routine where you'd go into the drugstore and you'd say, "I'd like two notepads, and some Lifesavers, and a tube of Ben-Gay, and (whispering) a condom," and the pharmacist screams at the top of his lungs, *"He wants to buy some rubbers!"* and everyone in the store turned and looked at you as if you had tertiary syphilis. And the irony was that you were just going to put it in your wallet. You had no idea how to use it—you didn't know which aperture it was to go into, or what appurtenance it was to go onto, but you always carried a rubber because that was what an adult male did. But it was about as appropriate in my virginal existence as a mastodon carrying a toothbrush.

So by the time I got married I was not much more worldly. And I went from that marriage to a rebound marriage, then I went about ten years as a bachelor and by that time I'd been around and I'd seen a few things and should have been expected to function better, but I was struck by what Mario Puzo calls "the thunderbolt": my third wife walked into a room, and I said, "I'm going to marry her," and like a schmuck I went and did it. The fourth marriage just sort of happened: It seemed like a good idea at the time. In fact—and this is the core of all my wisdom about love—whenever we try to explain why we have done any particular thing, whether it's buying T-bills or why we wound up living in a house in the mountains or why we took the trip to Lake Ronkonkoma, or whatever it was, the only rationale that ever rings with honesty is: "It seemed like a good idea at the time." We're really no smarter than cactus or wolverines or plankton; and the things we do, we always like to justify them, find logical reasons for them; and then you go to court later and the judge says, "Well, didn't you know that it was doomed from the start?" I'm waiting for someone to say to the judge, "Because, schmuck, I'm no smarter than you."

JW: *When and where did you lose your virginity?*

HE: The site of my defloration was on a couch in my mother's apartment at 12701 Shaker Boulevard in Cleveland, Ohio. Along about 1952–53, something like that. It was after my father had died and my mother and I had moved to Shaker Heights. I once asked the young woman in question whether I could write a piece about it—she was a virgin, I was a virgin, this was years later and she'd been married three times since—and I said to her, "Hey, I'd really like to write a piece about it because it was so funny." She said, "Don't you dare, I'll sue you." So I can't tell you her name but she was a science-fiction fan and I was a science-fiction fan and we were both young and covered with pimples and one night we just keep groping and groping until there was wet. It was like a docking maneuver in *2001: A Space Odyssey.*

JW: *Are Europeans more sophisticated about love?*

HE: When I came back from Paris Tom Snyder had me on the *Tomorrow* show and he asked me how I liked the French, and I said we ought to nuke 'em till they glow. This is a race, according to Charles de Gaulle, that "will only be united under the threat of danger. Nobody can simply bring together a country that has 265 kinds of cheese." The French are, as a *nation,* okay; but most of those who live in Paris, to be fair about it, are pond slime. These people don't just hate Americans, they hate the British, they despise Arabs, they loathe the Swiss, the Japanese, the Germans— they *really* hate Germans, they hate everybody. They hate somebody from the next arrondissement, fer Pete's sake! They are detestably loathsome; and they think—in that apt phrase we all learned in junior high school—they think their shit don't stink. And these are people who only discovered dry cleaning in the last five years. They wear heavy sweaters, they sweat like crazy in 'em, they don't shave their armpits, the sweat dries in the sweater, they put it on, and they go into a hot room, and they smell like the south end of a northbound horse. And they brag about love and romance, but it's basically a need to get the other person out of those sweaty clothes so you can breathe. The fucking is just an afterthought, just to keep busy while naked. I don't think they're any more sophisticated than we are.

JW: *What about the Oriental approach?*

HE: That's a different matter. I think Orientals do understand. They're much wiser. They're subtler. They have taken the time . . . they've placed the *value* there, at least until recently: Now Japan is an American suburb, it's Garden Grove East. They've spent the days of their heritage on aesthetics. The reason that, it seems to me, Orientals are better and wiser in sex and love is a manifestation of the same spirit that produced the Zen garden. Their religion is a much kinder religion than ours; it honors the forefathers, their gods are not mean-spirited, nasty, gimlet-eyed gods who'll give you a bolt of lightning in the ass if you masturbate.

JW: *You must have dated some between marriages. What have you learned about it?*

HE: I've learned not to put up with bad manners or bullshit. If I met a woman somewhere—a secretary, say—and she appealed to me, and I didn't have the chance to get to know her first and we went out and she began acting badly—by badly I mean a woman who didn't like the restaurant for an arbitrary reason, or she was complaining endlessly, a kvetch, or a person who was clearly mean-spirited—I would not put up with it. I would say, "Look, this date is not working out, you don't like me, I don't like you, and we're going to like each other a lot less as the evening goes on; so I'm taking you home now." I would take her home and that would be it. This assumes, of course, that I was every woman's fever-dream of the Perfect Date.

JW: *What kind of response would you receive?*

HE: Invariably the response would be uptight and icy. What do you expect? Women are not used to being treated that way. They're used either to being treated well by men or badly by men. There are guys who look at other women when they're out on a date; guys who grope; guys who are coarse or insensitive or racist or just plain stupid; guys who don't consider their date's wishes . . . and somehow, miraculously, these guys always get dates. God knows why, but beast-mentalities like these always seem to find female victims to brutalize, but always get dates. Contrariwise, there are guys who are really just human dishrags. They'll do whatever the woman pushes them to do; they don't have any sense of themselves. Bland is no protection. I'm an intelligent human being, and I expect the person I'm out with to be an intelligent human being; and if she's not, I treat her as if she is, nonetheless, and if she doesn't respond in kind, I just say, "This is not a profitable way for us to spend an evening." I only have *x* amount of life in my body, only *x* number of days in my life, and I simply don't have the time to spend not being enriched.

JW: *What's the worst date you've ever had?*

HE: In the twenty-six years I've lived in L.A. I've only met two phonies in Hollywood. Only two. I've met people whom I despise for one or another ethical reason . . . and a lot of people who were bad . . . and a lot of a people who lied . . . but to those who resonated the real definition of a "phony"—someone who's pretending to be something they aren't—only two. And one of them was a woman whom I met when she called to solicit me to go on *The Merv Griffin Show*. Now, the idea of going on *The Merv Griffin Show* was as alien, and as appealing to me, as a hysterectomy. But she had the most wonderful, mellifluous voice. She had an English accent, which I'm a sucker for (my wife, in self-fulfillment of this aberration, is English, with the accent), and I agreed to go on this dreadful, idiot show to sit there and talk to a man who has all the personality of a speed bump, because I was interested in this woman.

JW: *Based on the voice?*

HE: Based entirely on the voice and this charming conversation we had. She was bright, she was antic, she was—now this happened about ten years ago, so I was already in my middle forties, and she was a woman in her late thirties, maybe early forties—she was an *adult* woman. So I made a date with her for that night after the show. When I met her at the studio she was quite charming and very attractive—the voice fit the body. And I thought: This is wonderful, finally the illusion matches up with the reality.

Well, she wanted to double—she had a friend and wanted to know did I have someone to fix her friend up with. It just chanced that there was a guy who had come to visit from back East, a fairly charming, good-looking young guy, so I said yes, I'll bring a friend. So we went out.

Well, she didn't stop kvetching from the moment we got out. We went to the Pacific Dining Car for dinner and she kept calling it "one of those chophouses." I said, "Lady, when abalone is forty dollars a plate this ain't a 'chophouse.' " The Pacific Dining Car is a very nice and a very elegant restaurant. Has been for decades. She bitched and bitched and bitched and I was getting angrier and angrier and angrier. Had we been alone I simply would have said, "This is not working, I'm going to pay the check, here's enough for a cab, good-bye." We got in the car and we were coming back on the Hollywood Freeway—I'm driving, she's in the front seat, my friend and her friend are in the back—and as we drove through Hollywood she said, "Aghh, look at the filth, look at the squalor—we don't have this in London." London is filthy! And she went on and on and on. Nothing satisfied her: The restaurant had been too hot; the car seats were too low; the food had not pleased her; my clothes were not right; the moon was too full . . . she couldn't stop. As we were riding on the Hollywood Freeway, at about Gower, it reached absolute surface tension for me and I said: "Look, enough is enough. I don't know what your problem is, but I have taken you out for a nice meal, I'm an intelligent person, I'm a kindly person, I've been nice to you, I fixed up your friend . . . but you have not stopped bitching since the moment we got in this car."

"What do you mean? How dare you speak to me like that?"

"I speak to you thus because you are acting like a beast—and I cannot stand this and if you don't stop this behavior at once, one of us is getting the fuck out of this car and I don't really care whether it's you or me. *One* of us is getting the hell out of here! *Now* do you understand?"

She says, "Pull over, pull over!" So just before we got to the Highland exit I pulled onto the berm and I said, "Great; one of us is vacating this vehicle now!" And I started to open the door, to get out, to abandon my own car just to get away from this phony pain in the ass, but she opened her door and *she* stepped out because *she* was going to be the one to show *me*. I said, "Right!" and I slammed the door and took off, leaving her on the Hollywood Freeway. I may burn in hell for such irrational behavior, but sometimes one must simply act berserk to relocate oneself for sanity!

I take no pride in this, and in fact I feel some chagrin that I was driven to the point of lunacy where I couldn't physically bear to be in her presence. It was like being in Dachau. The evil of it was just too awful. The woman in the backseat was screaming, "Oh, you've abandoned her, you've abandoned her!" And my friend was hiding his face. I took them home, and that was the end of it. I simply could not bear to be in the presence of someone that mean, that rude, that awful! And I don't think anyone should be. But I deserve what I got, because my reasons for wanting to meet the woman were shallow, or they were dopily romantic, which is the same thing. Romantic, of necessity, is shallow.

JW: *Have you arrived at any kind of a definition of romantic love?*

HE: Sure, I can be as pedantic as anyone: Romantic love is the cloud of perfume through which you pass when you're in a movie theater, and it reminds you of an aunt who hugged you when you were three years old. It's as transitory as that, it's as ephemeral as that; it's as unrecapturable as that. Then we take this nebulosity, and we try to fit reality into it. We try to infuse this dream-mist into the fact that we are married to someone and we demand that they cook for us, we demand that they support us in everything, we demand that they be wiser and more sensitive than we, and yet they have no real, equal voice in the relationship. There're probably the equivalents of these things—irrational and debasing as they are—on the female side. The concept of romantic love is what gets in the way of happiness. It truly always poisons the well, because it makes the received world seem lackluster or inadequate by comparison.

JW: *Can you distinguish passion from romantic love?*

HE (suddenly breaking into an imitation of Mel Brooks as the 2000-Year-Old Man): Passion would be . . . when you look at someone and suddenly your mouth begins to water and your nose runs and you throw up on your toes and you jump on them and cover all of their exposed parts with saliva . . . would be passion. Romantic love would be neater, less messy, a lot drier.

JW: *Are passion and marriage irreconcilable?*

HE: I think so; at least *sustained* passion, the deranged blood-fever. What was Lautrec's great aphorism, "Marriage is like a very long meal, with the dessert at the beginning"? Marriage is intended to do one thing and passion is intended to do something else. Passion is intended to flare and burn for an instant, to sear your intellect and your emotions. It's a rush, it's like catching the seventh wave. Marriage is intended to sustain you, to keep you sane and keep you whole and provide a schema that enables you to enjoy the blinding, exhausting moments of passion when they come. Marriage is the superstructure of the building; passion is the elevator.

JW: *You seem to be saying that love is sustained in marriage by accommodation on the part of both parties. Has your wife adapted to your life-style?*

HE: That's what I meant when I said it was a miracle. Sans hyperbole, Susan is a saint. I'm impossible to live with. But she battens on it; she actually enjoys being in my company all day, sunup to bedtime. We've been together three years, married for two—which is longer than three of my marriages put together—and with minor breaks, we haven't been out of each other's sight in all that time. And there has never, in my entire life, been *anyone,* no matter how much they liked me, including my parents, who could stand to be in my company for more than half an hour. I'm not exaggerating. I'm an incredibly wearing person to be around. Let me give you a footnote on this. Brother Theodore, who is a friend of mine, is one of the wisest and most wonderful people in the world, sadly undervalued and tragically not a household name. Anyway, when we first met we sat and talked for hours. Teddy is in his eighties, and after a few hours he said to me [imitating Brother Theodore], "You know, Harlan, we are very much alike, you and I, very much alike in one way. It is the reason women run *shrieking* from us. When they meet us, at first we are full of life and passion and intensity, and they are attracted to this. It is dangerous. They say, 'Ah, there is something alive here' and they seek that heat and they get involved with us and it goes on for a week and then a month and then six months and then a year and they say, 'When will it *end*? When will it *stop*? When will there be some *peace*? When will there be some *quiet*?' And there is none, so they run *shrieking* from us."

That's precisely what has happened to me all through my life: Every relationship I've had, even the best of them, even where I was able to remain good friends with the woman afterwards—and I have many friendships like that—they eventually came and, with great weariness, said "I can take no more." Or they would just say, "I'm leaving, *schmuck*," and they would go. With Susan it's a situation that I have never had before; and it's the basis at least for *my* happiness. God knows what demented pleasure *she* derives from the marriage—the woman must be totally deranged to be so happy in this relationship—but the basis for *my* happiness is that I love being in her company and she seems to enjoy *my* company. Go figure.

I wake up late at night. I sleep a lot more lightly than Susan—my wife is one of the great sleepers, she's an Olympic dozer, an *intense* sleeper, she nests, she rolls over, she gets into it—but I'll wake up and I'll look at her face in repose, and I'm filled with the most astonishing molasses. I stare at that face and say to myself, "I have done something right, somewhere in my life, to have been accorded that moment in which we met." The chances of meeting that person are so slim. I wrote a story about true love called "Grail" that makes its point in the old Chinese adage that the great tragedy of life is that my one true friend died six years before I was born, and that my one true love will not come along until six years after I am dead. So for the parts to have meshed, particularly in a case as difficult as mine, is a miracle. There is tenderness and compassion in our relationship and the passion happens at odd moments, and that's fine.

JW: *Do you think men and women respond to pornography differently?*

HE: I don't know, I'm not a woman. I read the studies that say that women respond in slightly different ways than men, but I don't even think two *men* respond the same way. I don't think any two *people* respond the same way. When I was editing *Rogue* magazine, we would get packs of photos of naked women from which to pick a photo spread. You'd look at literally thousands of photographs of women, most of them on slides, and you'd be looking at them in extreme close-up, where every pubic hair was in clear definition and after a while it was not that you became bored, it was that you became disinterested, because there are only a limited number of variations of the human body. Then you'd be going along and suddenly you would hit a shot and you would say, "Wow," and your legs would twitch for a moment and you would say, "Now that's a great photo." And you would put it aside, but if you really looked at it, it was precisely the same pose as a thousand others you had seen. So you would ask yourself, "Why in the world did that one get me?" Well, if you studied it long enough, and I did, invariably it would be a curvilinear arch of the foot; it would be the edge of a smile; it would be the way a head was turned in design with the neck; invariably it would be something aesthetic. There was nothing sexual about it, it was that aesthetic thing that you were looking it. And when you look at Las Vegas dancers or cheerleaders when they're doing their numbers, they'll hit a pose and the hip will cock out a certain way and the leg will be tilted another way and you say, "That one turns me on." And no two people see it the same way.

JW: *What about the question, "What do women want?"*

HE: It's not monolithic: What one woman wants is not what another woman wants. For instance, I find it very hard to be violent with women. I've led a violent life myself: My response to film producers who give me a hard time is to punch them. But when I hear about guys who beat up women or who molest children, my head explodes and I say, "How can such people be?" I know there are amoral, sociopathic types, there are people who are demented, there are people who were abused themselves, but it is very alien to me. So I have never been able to get very much behind a relationship in which the woman demanded that I be physically violent. In the past, some women would say, "Hurt me a little, hurt me a little," when we were having sex. Pressed to it, I'd always try, awkwardly, but I always felt uncomfortable; and I never quite gave them what they wanted. In fact, in one of my books, *Stalking the Nightmare*, there's a piece called "The 3 Most Important Things in Life": my most bizarre sexual escapade, the most violent thing that ever happened to me, and a piece about the time I worked for Disney for three hours before they fired me. The sexual thing is really hilarious *now*, because I tell it hilariously, but when it was happening, it was frightening to me that a woman was asking me to debase her or to bind her in some way.

JW: *What turned you off about it?*

HE: The thing that turned me off about it is very clear to me; I prize above all other things in this life my personal space, my dignity, however little it may be—I'm not a very dignified guy but I have a sense of "You may go this far and no further." I am affronted that my publisher has changed the size of my book without asking me: they have invaded a venue to which I have never given them admittance. This woman was not only willingly but anxiously *demanding* that I demean her, that I reduce not just her living space but the infinite quality of her humanity so that she could get off by thinking she was not worthy—this gets very confusing and it's so goddamn Freudian—she was not treating herself as well as she should have been treating herself.

JW: *One last question: What have you learned about love and marriage?*

HE (as the 2000-Year-Old-Man again): The one thing you learn about love is that it's like ice skating: If you don't have the ankles, don't try it. [Pauses, now as himself] The one thing that I know about love for sure is that it's the only game in town and that you must keep going back to bat again and again and again. I have no respect for anyone who says they've given up, or that they're not looking or that they're tired. That is to abrogate one's responsibility as a human being.

HARLAN ELLISON is an award-winning novelist and screenwriter. His most recent book is *Angry Candy*.

ᕇ THE WAR BETWEEN ᕇ
MEN AND WOMEN

There will always be a battle between the sexes
because men and women want different things.
Men want women and women want men.

GEORGE BURNS

Relations between the sexes are so complicated
that the only way you can tell if two members of
the set are "going together" is if they are married.
Then, almost certainly, they are not.

CLEVELAND AMORY

A man defending husbands vs. wives or men vs.
women has got about as much chance as a traffic
policeman trying to stop a mad dog by blowing
two whistles.   RING LARDNER

The war between the sexes is the only one in
which both sides regularly sleep with the enemy.

QUENTIN CRISP

The first time Adam had a chance, he laid the
blame on women.   NANCY ASTOR

In the sex-war thoughtlessness is the weapon of
the male, vindictiveness of the female.

CYRIL CONNOLLY

Beware of the man who
denounces women writers;
his penis is tiny & cannot spell.   ERICA JONG

> Girls have an unfair advantage over men: if they
> can't get what they want by being smart, they can
> get it by being dumb.   YUL BRYNNER

Heinrich Heine bequeathed his estate to his wife on the condition that
she marry again, because, according to Heine, "There will be at least one
man who will regret my death."

All the reasons of man cannot outweigh a single
feeling of a woman.   VOLTAIRE

> We study ourselves three weeks, we love each
> other three months, we squabble three years, we
> tolerate each other thirty years, and then the chil-
> dren start all over again.   HIPPOLYTE TAINE

She looks like Lady Chatterley above the waist
and the gamekeeper below.
        CYRIL CONNOLLY on Vita Sackville-West

A woman whose face looked as if it had been made of sugar and someone had licked it.
GEORGE BERNARD SHAW on Isadora Duncan

Madame de Genlis, in order to avoid the scandal of coquetry, always yielded easily.   TALLEYRAND

Erica Jong wrote in *Fear of Flying*: "The zipless fuck is absolutely pure . . . and it is rarer than the unicorn." Before attending a book convention, Jong asked the poet Anne Sexton for advice: "What do I do when men come up to me . . . and say, 'Hey baby, I want a zipless fuck'?" Anne Sexton replied, "Thank them and say 'Zip up your fuck until I ask for it.' "

She has a double chin and an overdeveloped chest and she's rather short in the leg. So I can hardly describe her as the most beautiful creature I've ever seen. RICHARD BURTON on Elizabeth Taylor

She was the type that would wake up in the morning and *immediately* start apologizing.
WOODY ALLEN

She's the original good time that was had by all.
BETTE DAVIS

She's been on more laps than a napkin.
WALTER WINCHELL

Alcestis had exercised a mysterious attraction and then an unmysterious repulsion on two former husbands, the second of whom had to resort to fatal coronary disease to get away from her.

KINGSLEY AMIS

It is not true that I dated Al Goldstein.

TONI GRANT

A man who has never made a woman angry is a failure in life. CHRISTOPHER MORLEY

No man is a match for a woman, except with a poker and a hobnailed pair of boots—and not always even then. GEORGE BERNARD SHAW

She was so glad to see me go, that I have almost a mind to come again, that she may again have the same pleasure. SAMUEL JOHNSON

The concern that some women show at the absence of their husbands does not arise from their not seeing them and being with them, but from the apprehension that their husbands are enjoying pleasures in which they do not participate, and which, from their being at a distance, they have not the power of interrupting. MONTAIGNE

When men and women agree, it is only in their conclusions; their reasons are always different.

SANTAYANA

Never go to bed mad. Stay up and fight.

PHYLLIS DILLER

It is hard to fight an enemy who has outposts in your head.   SALLY KEMPTON

As far as I'm concerned, being any gender is a drag.   PATTI SMITH

❖━━━━━━━━━━━━━━━━━━━━━━━━❖

Toscanini, displeased with the singing of a soprano during a rehearsal, grabbed her by the breasts and screamed, "If only these were brains!"

❖━━━━━━━━━━━━━━━━━━━━━━━━❖

The only position for women in SNCC is prone.   STOKELY CARMICHAEL

When women discovered the orgasm it was, combined with modern birth control, perhaps the biggest single nail in the coffin of male dominance.   EVA FIGES

Between men and women there is no friendship possible. There is passion, enmity, worship, love, but no friendship.   OSCAR WILDE

I don't believe man is woman's natural enemy. Perhaps his lawyer is.   SHANA ALEXANDER

Most hierarchies were established by men who now monopolize the upper levels, thus depriving women of their rightful share of opportunities for incompetence.   LAURENCE PETER

One day, an army of gray-haired women may
quietly take over the earth.   GLORIA STEINEM

>   Nobody will ever win the battle of the sexes.
There's too much fraternizing with the enemy.
                                        HENRY KISSINGER

On a visit to the United States, Winston Churchill attended a
luncheon where fried chicken was served. When he politely asked the
hostess, "May I have more breast?" she scolded him: "Mr. Churchill, in
America we say 'white meat' or 'dark meat.' " The next day Churchill
sent the woman an orchid with the following note: "Madam, I would be
much obliged if you would pin this on your white meat."

FIELD MARSHAL MONTGOMERY: Lady Astor, I must
tell you that I do not approve of politicians.
LADY ASTOR: That's all right. The only general I
approve of is Evangeline Booth.

              BESSIE BRADDOCK: Winston, you're drunk!
WINSTON CHURCHILL: Bessie, you're ugly. But
tomorrow I shall be sober.

LADY ASTOR: If you were my husband, Winston,
I'd put poison in your tea.
WINSTON CHURCHILL: If I were your husband,
Nancy, I'd drink it.

LADY RUMPERS: And then you took me.
SIR PERCY: I took *you*? You took *me*. Your Land Army breeches came down with a fluency born of long practice.   ALAN BENNETT

MALE HECKLER: Are you a lesbian?
FLORYNCE KENNEDY: Are you my alternative?

NOEL COWARD: Why, Edna, you look almost like a man in that suit.
EDNA FERBER: So do you, Noel, so do you.

PRINCE OF WALES: I've spent enough on you to buy a battleship.
LILLIE LANGTRY: And you've spent enough *in* me to float one.

It is easier to be a lover than a husband for the simple reason that it is more difficult to be witty every day than to produce the occasional *bon mot*.
BALZAC

Husbands are chiefly good lovers when they are betraying their wives. MARILYN MONROE

American women expect to find in their husbands a perfection that English women only hope to find in their butlers. W. SOMERSET MAUGHAM

American husbands are the best in the world; no other husbands are so generous to their wives, or can be so easily divorced. ELINOR GLYN

The only way a woman can ever reform her husband is by boring him so completely that he loses all possible interest in life. OSCAR WILDE

Husbands are awkward things to deal with; even keeping them in hot water will not make them tender. MARY BUCKLEY

Husbands think we should know where everything is—like the uterus is a tracking device. He asks me, "Roseanne, do we have any Chee-tos left?" Like he can't go over to that sofa cushion and lift it himself. ROSEANNE BARR

We wedded men live in sorrow and care.
CHAUCER

Intelligent women always marry fools.
ANATOLE FRANCE

It is necessary to be almost a genius to make a good husband.　BALZAC

Being a husband is a whole-time job. That is why so many husbands fail. They cannot give their entire attention to it.　ARNOLD BENNETT

There isn't a wife in the world who has not taken the exact measure of her husband, weighed him and settled him in her own mind, and knows him as well as if she had ordered him after designs and specifications of her own.
CHARLES DUDLEY WARNER

I think every woman is entitled to a middle husband she can forget.　ADELA ROGERS ST. JOHN

Before marriage, a man declares that he would lay down his life to serve you; after marriage, he won't even lay down his newspaper to talk to you.
HELEN ROWLAND

When you consider what a chance women have to poison their husbands, it's a wonder there isn't more of it done.　KIN HUBBARD

If women believed in their husbands they would be a good deal happier—and also a good deal more foolish.　H. L. MENCKEN

One exists with one's husband—one lives with one's lover.　BALZAC

[Married men] are horribly tedious when they are good husbands, and abominably conceited when they are not.   OSCAR WILDE

Husbands are like fires—they go out when un-attended.   ZSA ZSA GABOR

A bachelor has to have inspiration for making love to a woman, a married man needs only an excuse.
                                HELEN ROWLAND

I know many married men, I even know a few happily married men, but I don't know one who wouldn't fall down the first open coal-hole run-ning after the first pretty girl who gave him a wink.   GEORGE JEAN NATHAN

If there were no husbands, who would look after our mistresses?   GEORGE MOORE

The average woman must inevitably view her ac-tual husband with a certain disdain; he is anything but her ideal. In consequence, she cannot help feeling that her children are cruelly handicapped by the fact that he is their father.
                                H. L. MENCKEN

The American girl makes a servant of her husband and then finds him contemptible for being a servant.
                                JOHN STEINBECK

If you cannot have your dear husband for a com-fort and a delight, for a breadwinner and a cross-patch, for a sofa, chair or hot water bottle, one can use him as a Cross to be borne.
                                STEVIE SMITH

ᔐ ALICE KAHN ᔑ

JW: *What are the essential differences between men and women?*
AK (laughing): I just asked Herb Caen that and he said, "Do you want me to draw you a picture?" What are the differences between men and women? As my high school biology teacher used to say, "What is sex? Ovaries and testes, egg cells and sperm cells." And pants and skirts, I would add. I think culture follows anatomy. There are certain cultural experiences that come with the genitals.
JW: *Do you agree that marriage is a bankrupt institution?*
AK: No, I definitely don't, having been married twenty-two years

to my first and only husband. I think it's the best thing that ever happened in my life.

JW: *Then I guess you would disagree that passion and marriage are irreconcilable.*

AK: Yup.

JW: *If in fact passion requires obstacles and lack of opportunity and doom— how do you keep it alive in a marriage?*

AK: I don't think passion requires obstacles, I think it requires stimulation. Things happen in life that both heat you up and cool you down, both before and after you're married—perhaps not with the same intensity as when you're a teenager or when you meet somebody for the first time, but it ebbs and flows.

JW: *How would you characterize the state of the women's movement?*

AK: There's a "media" feminism, which is a very silly feminism that has to do with burning bras and insisting on trivialities like forms of address. And there's a deeper, more serious feminism which has had certain victories, one of which was the extension of a variety of reproductive rights for women including a wide range of birth-control and child-delivery options that were previously unavailable. I'm talking about everything from natural childbirth to clinics for teenage girls to legalized abortion.

JW: *What do you think of the idea that "People would never fall in love if they had not heard love talked about"?*

AK: Well, now you're getting into the whole Denis de Rougemont *Love in the Western World* idea that love was invented by European culture. It depends on where you want to draw the line between love and sex. I'm not sure, though, having always lived in a world where love was talked about. I'm not sure what the cave people thought of the whole thing. Maybe a couple of bumps and grinds and seed spillings were all there was to it for them, or maybe the cave women actually sat around writing "Johnny" with curlicues on the walls of the cave.

JW: *Do you think the current younger generation is worse off than its predecessors when it comes to love?*

AK: I do think they're at a disadvantage because of all the evils that have been unleashed in the last twenty years, specifically the ready availability of drugs and alcohol that alter people's minds and behavior and confuse you when you're already under the influence of powerful, naturally occurring drugs called hormones. And the existence and increasing presence of violent people and violent weapons in our world has complicated the search for love. And people make the whole thing harder than it has to be by being so civilized and out of touch with instinct.

JW: *How do we get more in touch with instinct?*

AK: Try to get as much done as possible while you're still a child.

ALICE KAHN is a nationally syndicated columnist and the author of *Multiple Sarcasm* and *My Life as a Gal*.

❧ INFIDELITY ❧

There are few who would not rather be taken in adultery than in provincialism.   ALDOUS HUXLEY

Accursed from their birth they be
Who seek to find monogamy.
Pursuing it from bed to bed—
I think they would be better dead.

DOROTHY PARKER

The psychology of adultery has been falsified by conventional morals, which assume, in monogamous countries, that attraction to one person cannot coexist with affection for another. Everybody knows that this is untrue.   BERTRAND RUSSELL

Sara could commit adultery at one end and weep for her sins at the other, and enjoy both operations at once.   JOYCE CARY

Viscount Waldorf Astor owned Britain's two most influential newspapers, *The Times* and the *Observer,* but his American wife, Nancy, had a wider circulation than both papers put together.

EMERY KELLEN

Your idea of fidelity is not having more than one man in bed at the same time.

DIRK BOGARDE in *Darling*
(screenplay by Frederic Raphael)

Heiresses are never jilted.   GEORGE MEREDITH

You cannot pluck roses without fear of thorns,
nor enjoy a fair wife without danger of horns.
BENJAMIN FRANKLIN

You can't tell your friend you've been cuckolded;
even if he doesn't laugh at you, he may put the
information to personal use.   MONTAIGNE

The lover thinks of possessing his mistress more
often than her husband thinks of guarding his
wife.   STENDHAL

I am a strict monogamist: it is twenty years since I
last went to bed with two women at once, and
then I was in my cups and not myself.
H. L. MENCKEN

When a woman unhappily yoked talks about the
soul with a man not her husband, it isn't the soul
they are talking about.   DON MARQUIS

As we all know from witnessing the consuming
jealousy of husbands who are never faithful, people do not confine themselves to the emotions to
which they are entitled.   QUENTIN CRISP

Few things in life are more embarrassing than the
necessity of having to inform an old friend that
you have just got engaged to his fiancee.
W. C. FIELDS

A man does not look behind the door unless he
has stood there himself.   HENRI DU BOIS

GEORGE S. KAUFMAN: I like your bald head, Marc. It feels just like my wife's behind.
MARC CONNOLLY (feeling his pate): So it does, George, so it does.

When a Roman was returning from a trip, he used to send someone ahead to let his wife know, so as not to surprise her in the act.   MONTAIGNE

There are women whose infidelities are the only link they still have with their husbands.
SACHA GUITRY

I am not faithful but I am attached.
GÜNTER GRASS

Adultery is the application of democracy to love.
H. L. MENCKEN

Benchley and I had an office in the old *Life* magazine that was so tiny, if it were an inch smaller it would have been adultery.   DOROTHY PARKER

Even in civilized mankind faint traces of monogamous instinct can be perceived.
BERTRAND RUSSELL

When a man steals your wife, there is no better revenge than to let him keep her.
SACHA GUITRY

I've been in love with the same woman for forty-one years. If my wife finds out, she'll kill me.
HENNY YOUNGMAN

A Code of Honor: Never approach a friend's girl-friend or wife with mischief as your goal. There are just too many women in the world to justify that sort of dishonorable behavior. Unless she's *really* attractive.　BRUCE JAY FRIEDMAN

My boyfriend and I broke up. He wanted to get married, and I didn't want him to.

RITA RUDNER

The woman who is about to deceive her husband always carefully thinks out how she is going to act, but she is never logical.　BALZAC

Never tell. Not if you love your wife . . . In fact, if your old lady walks in on you deny it. Yeah. Just flat out and she'll believe it: "I'm tellin' ya. This chick came downstairs with a sign around her neck "Lay On Top Of Me Or I'll Die." I didn't know what I was gonna do . . .　LENNY BRUCE

Women want you to deceive them: they force you to, and if you resist, they blame you.　FLAUBERT

I told my wife the truth. I told her I was seeing a psychiatrist. Then she told *me* the truth: that she was seeing a psychiatrist, two plumbers and a bartender.　RODNEY DANGERFIELD

☙ TRUE CONFESSIONS ❧

I've looked on a lot of women with lust. I've committed adultery in my heart many times. This is something God recognizes I will do, and God forgives me for it.   JIMMY CARTER

I have never loved anyone for love's sake, except, perhaps, Josephine—a little.   NAPOLEON I

I never loved another person the way I loved myself.   MAE WEST

I love the bitch to death.   KEITH RICHARDS on his wife

Music is my mistress, and she plays second fiddle to no one.   DUKE ELLINGTON

I love Mickey Mouse more than any woman I've ever known.   WALT DISNEY

I like young girls. Their stories are shorter.   THOMAS McGUANE

I belong to Bridegrooms Anonymous. Whenever I feel like getting married, they send over a lady in a housecoat and hair curlers to burn my toast for me.   DICK MARTIN

For the first year of marriage I had a basically bad attitude. I tended to place my wife underneath a pedestal.   WOODY ALLEN

I hate to be a failure. I hate and regret the failure of my marriages. I would gladly give all my millions for just one lasting marital success.

J. PAUL GETTY

I didn't know how babies were made until I was pregnant with my fourth child five years later.

LORETTA LYNN

I would rather score a touchdown than make love to the prettiest girl in the United States.

PAUL HORNUNG

I would rather go to bed with Lillian Russell stark naked than Ulysses S. Grant in full military regalia.

MARK TWAIN

If it weren't for pickpockets, I'd have no sex life at all. RODNEY DANGERFIELD

I go out with actresses because I'm not apt to marry one. HENRY KISSINGER

I have never hated a man enough to give his diamonds back. ZSA ZSA GABOR

I wanted to be called Mr. March.

BURT REYNOLDS on why he posed nude for *Cosmopolitan*

When I was young, I used to have successes with women because I was young. Now I have successes with woman because I am old. Middle age was the hardest part. ARTHUR RUBINSTEIN

Once they call you a Latin Lover, you're in real trouble. Women expect an Oscar performance in bed. MARCELLO MASTROIANNI

Sex appeal is fifty percent what you've got and fifty percent what people think you've got.
SOPHIA LOREN

As a young man I used to have four supple members and one stiff one. Now I have four stiff and one supple. HENRI, DUC D'AUMALE

If I hadn't had them, I would have had some made. DOLLY PARTON

I have never been able to sleep with anyone. I require a full-size bed so that I can lie in the middle of it and extend my arms spreadeagle on both sides without being obstructed. MAE WEST

I didn't get ahead by sleeping with people. Girls, take heart! BARBARA WALTERS

I've only slept with the men I've been married to. How many women can make that claim?
ELIZABETH TAYLOR

I should never have married, but I didn't want to live without a man. Brought up to respect the conventions, love had to end in marriage. I'm afraid it did. BETTE DAVIS

The vast majority of women who pretend vaginal orgasms are faking it to "get the job."
TI-GRACE ATKINSON

Personally, I like sex and I don't care what a man thinks of me as long as I get what I want from him—which is usually sex.   VALERIE PERRINE

I've never taken up with a congressman in my life
. . . I've never gone below the Senate.
BARBARA HOWAR

All a writer has to do to get a woman is to say he's a writer. It's an aphrodisiac.   SAUL BELLOW

Being baldpate is an unfailing sex magnet.
TELLY SAVALAS

I tell the women that the face is my experience and the hands are my soul—anything to get those panties down.   CHARLES BUKOWSKI

ఈ MARTIN MULL ఈ

JW: *What's your definition of romantic love?*

MM: It would have to be the opposite of business.

JW: *Do you think love is culturally conditioned?*

MM: If it wasn't for television and movies, people might easily kiss with their feet.

JW: *Is there a difference between the portrayal of love in movies versus television?*

MM: Yes, television portrays love with no hair on it—it's been airbrushed away.

JW: *Is marriage a realistic institution?*

MM: It's a logical progression of the human condition; for many it's the only chance to have, depending on your sex, a mother or father you can actually talk to. A man will marry a woman because he needs a mother he can communicate with. There are other roles, of course: sister, lover, girlfriend, wife.

JW: *What about the idea that passion and marriage can't coexist?*

MM: It depends on what kind of passion you're talking about. There are married couples who become extremely passionate about remodeling. If you're talking about *lustful* passion, I don't know. Maybe it isn't realistic to expect marriage to do all the things that we expect it to, but then it isn't realistic to expect the Cleveland Browns to win the Super Bowl this year, yet I believe they will. I approach marriage with the same attitude, and I think I've come pretty close, or as close as I can handle, in my marriage. But you have to be very lucky.

JW: *What are the basic differences between men and women?*

MM: Men are essentially dogs and women are essentially cats. Men are more capable of sniffing a new acquaintance's asshole on the sidewalk. Women are *sleeker.*

JW: *Do you remember your all-time worst date?*

MM: Yes. It was about 1972. I was performing in nightclubs around the country, and as part of an attempt to drum up ticket sales, Warner Brothers Records, which was my distributor at the time, the local radio station, and the local club in Cleveland put together a "Win a Dream Date with Martin Mull" contest. You sent in a three-by-five postcard with just your name—because obviously any statement of "Why I Want a Date With Martin Mull" wouldn't take up a whole three-by-five card. They put the cards in what looked like a large hamster cage and at the appointed time the disc jockey turned them around and plucked one out.

It was won by three sisters who entered jointly. For joint custody. At that time my act was called "Martin Mull and His Fabulous Furniture," which was basically myself, an easy chair, an end table, and a lamp. We packed up the furniture in the back of a pickup truck and sort of arranged them as best we could to look like a living room and went down to find these three people.

I arrived at the house with the guy from the record company, and to call it a lean-to shack would be giving it too much credit. It was in the blast-furnace section of Cleveland, down near the smelting pits of the steel works. Instead of a backyard there were smokestacks spewing out flames. I knocked on the door and a man answered who looked like Walter Brennan's understudy. He had one of those white-haired beards that's like a Don Johnson beard, but on an older man it takes on a whole different quality.

I said, "Hello, my name is Martin Mull and I believe your daughters are having a date with me tonight." The date was going to consist of going to a certain part of town, watching the lights change, and going to McDonald's. All very funny.

One of the girls finally comes down the stairs and says, "Martin, we can't go," and bursts into tears, followed by the other two girls, equally red-eyed. The father says, "They just found out an hour ago that their mother has cancer, so they're not going out."

I'm sitting there with more egg on my face than I could ever imagine, and the fucking guy from Warner Brothers tries to make light of it by saying, "Cancer, really? I'm an Aries!" There was, of course, no laugh forthcoming. I was dying. Then he said, "Hey, only kiddin'—I know how you must feel and it's a shame you can't go, but here are some free albums." He gave them three long-playing record albums of, I think, the Doobie Brothers, the Allman Brothers and whatever other brothers they had. That was the end of my dream date.

JW: *You only met the one girl?*

MM: I only met the one, yes. The other two were sobbing in the background like a Greek chorus. It was grim. The fortunate thing was, just in case it didn't pan out, just in case these three young ladies weren't exactly the final three of the Miss Universe Pageant, I took the added precaution of bringing my own date, who sat in the cab of the pickup. Since the three sisters were unable to go, she made her way to the back of the truck and we went out and watched the lights change and then went to McDonald's.

JW: *Do you read "relationship" books?*

MM: You mean books like *Women Who Beat the Crap Out of Husbands and Husbands Who Let Them Do It?* These books do nothing but stir up trouble. They appeal to people who are disturbed by telling them, "You are not disturbed, you are simply confused." Disturbed and confused are very different things. The books allow them to label their various shortcomings and aggressions as righteous, and given that the Bible is still a big seller, doesn't that in a way fall under the same heading as those books like *How to Be Your Own Next-door Neighbor?*

JW: *In your book,* The History of White People in America, *you say, "Fun is contrary to the whole concept of white sex." If that's true, what's the attraction?*

MM: The fear of leaving your money to the state.

JW: *Last question: What do women want?*

MM: They want to be Mrs. Kevin Costner. Mention his name around any woman between the ages of twenty and eighty-five and they drool. They love him. He's the ladies' man of the eighties—or the second half of the eighties—or the second half of '88—or the Ladies' Man du Jour.

Actually, I think a lot of women want to be somewhere between Mother Teresa and Lee Iacocca.

MARTIN MULL is an actor/writer/comedian and the coauthor of *A Paler Shade of White.*

﴾ KISSING ﴿

Lord! I wonder what fool it was that first invented kissing. JONATHAN SWIFT

> To a woman the first kiss is just the end of the
> beginning but to a man it is the beginning of the
> end. HELEN ROWLAND

The first kiss is stolen by the man; the last is
begged by the woman. H. L. MENCKEN

> I will not have my face smeared with lipstick. If
> you want to kiss me, kiss me on the lips, which is
> what a merciful providence provided them for.
> HERBERT MARSHALL in *The Razor's Edge*
> (screenplay by Lamar Trotti, from the
> novel by W. Somerset Maugham)

Oh, what lies there are in kisses.
HEINRICH HEINE

> Two people kissing always look like fish.
> ANDY WARHOL

I'd love to kiss you, but I just washed my hair.
BETTE DAVIS in *Cabin in the Cotton*
(screenplay by Paul Green)

> Kissing don't last; cookery do!
> GEORGE MEREDITH

In love there is always one who kisses and one
who offers the cheek.   FRENCH PROVERB

I wasn't kissing her, I was whispering in her mouth.
                                              CHICO MARX

Kissing and bussing differ in this:
We busse our Wantons, but our Wives
    we kisse.   ROBERT HERRICK

A word invented by the poets as a rhyme for
"bliss."   AMBROSE BIERCE

Everybody winds up kissing the wrong person
good night.   ANDY WARHOL

❧ LOVE ❧

Love is a universal migraine,
A bright stain on the vision,
Blotting out reason.   ROBERT GRAVES

Love is the child of illusion and the parent of
disillusion.   MIGUEL DE UNAMUNO

Love is like war: easy to begin but very hard to
stop.   H. L. MENCKEN

Love is a springtime plant that perfumes everything with its hope, even the ruins to which it
clings.   FLAUBERT

Love is the self-delusion we manufacture to justify
the trouble we take to have sex.
        DAN GREENBURG

A constant interrogation.   MILAN KUNDERA

A mutual misunderstanding.   OSCAR WILDE

The union of a want and a sentiment.   BALZAC

A narcissism shared by two.   RITA MAE BROWN

A game of secret, cunning stratagems, in which
only the fools who are fated to lose reveal their
true aims or motives—even to themselves.
        EUGENE O'NEILL

A sort of hostile transaction, very necessary to
keep the world going, but by no means a sinecure
to the parties concerned.   LORD BYRON

Love is an incurable malady like those pathetic states in which rheumatism affords the sufferer a brief respite only to be replaced by epileptiform headaches. MARCEL PROUST

The cure of coquetry. LA ROCHEFOUCAULD

Two minds without a single thought.
PHILIP BARRY

The drug which makes sexuality palatable in popular mythology. GERMAINE GREER

Love is the affection of a mind that has nothing better to engage it. THEOPHRASTUS

Love ain't nothing but sex misspelled.
HARLAN ELLISON

A grave mental disease. PLATO

Love is the irresistible desire to be irresistibly desired. ROBERT FROST

Something you have to make ... It's all work, work. JOYCE CARY

Something that never happens anywhere at any time. CHARLES BUKOWSKI

Desperate madness. JOHN FORD

Nothing else but an insatiate thirst of enjoying a greedily desired object. MONTAIGNE

Friendship is a disinterested commerce between equals; love, an abject intercourse between tyrants and slaves. OLIVER GOLDSMITH

Love is the selfishness of two persons. ANTOINE DE LA SALE

Love is . . . not a fact in nature of which we become aware, but rather a creation of the human imagination. JOSEPH WOOD KRUTCH

Love itself is the most elitist of passions. It acquires its stereoscopic substance and perspective only in the context of culture, for it takes up more place in the mind than it does in bed. Outside of that setting it falls flat into one-dimensional fiction. JOSEPH BRODSKY

Romantic love is mental illness. But it's a pleasurable one. It's a drug. It distorts reality, and that's the point of it. It would be impossible to fall in love with someone that you really *saw*. FRAN LEBOWITZ

I know what love is: Tracy and Hepburn, Bogart and Bacall, Romeo and Juliet, Jackie and John and Marilyn . . . IAN SHOALES

Where they love they do not desire and where they desire they do not love. SIGMUND FREUD

Love is like an hourglass, with the heart filling up
as the brain empties.   JULES RENARD

The most terrible thing of all is happy love, for
then there is fear in everything.

COSIMA WAGNER

What starts love is your ability to stupefy and
blind yourself to the point of being able to fall in
love. What stops it is waking up.

FRAN LEBOWITZ

The stellar universe is not so difficult to understand as the real actions of other people, especially
of the people with whom we are in love.

MARCEL PROUST

❖━━━━━━━━━━━━━━━━━━━━━━━━❖

George S. Kaufman told Irving Berlin that the lyrics to his song "Always" were unrealistic. Instead of "I'll be loving you, always," Kaufman
suggested: "I'll be loving you, Thursday."

❖━━━━━━━━━━━━━━━━━━━━━━━━❖

The word *relationship* best refers to the connection
between parasite and host, or shark and remora.
It's a biological term. I'd rather be a jerk than a
scientist when it comes to love.   IAN SHOALES

Love has no great influences upon the sum of life.

SAMUEL JOHNSON

Love has no heart.   NED ROREM

> If two people love each other there can be no
> happy end to it.   ERNEST HEMINGWAY

Love is more pleasant once you get out of your
twenties. It doesn't hurt all the time.
               ANDREW A. ROONEY

> When you're away, I'm restless, lonely,
> Wretched, bored, dejected; only
> Here's the rub, my darling dear,
> I feel the same when you are here.
>   SAMUEL HOFFENSTEIN

When you're in love it's the most glorious two-
and-a-half days of your life.   RICHARD LEWIS

> I hate and love. You ask, perhaps, how can that
> be?
>   I know not, but I feel the agony.   CATULLUS

If love is judged by most of its effects, it resembles
hate more than friendship.   LA ROCHEFOUCAULD

> Love is a reciprocity of soul and has a different
> end and obeys different laws from marriage. Hence
> one should not take the loved one to wife.
>   ALESSANDRO PICCOLOMINI

A ridiculous passion which hath no being but in
play-books and romances.   JONATHAN SWIFT

There is nothing good in love but the physical part. COMTE DE BUFFON

The contact of two epidermises.
SEBASTIEN CHAMFORT

An attempt to change a piece of a dream-world into reality. THEODORE REIK

Just another four-letter word.
TENNESSEE WILLIAMS

Everything we do in life is based on fear, especially love. MEL BROOKS

People would never fall in love if they had not heard love talked about. LA ROCHEFOUCAULD

There is hardly any activity, any enterprise, which is started with such tremendous hopes and expectations and yet which fails so regularly as love.
ERICH FROMM

Moved by a passion they do not understand for a goal they seldom reach, men and women are haunted by the vision of a distant possibility that refuses to be extinguished. NATHANIEL BRANDEN

Lovers who have nothing to do but love each other are not really to be envied; love and nothing else very soon is nothing else.
WALTER LIPPMANN

It is the whole modern conception of love which should be re-examined, such as is commonly but transparently expressed in phrases like "love at first sight" and "honeymoon." All this shoddy terminology is on top of that tainted with the most reactionary irony.   ANDRÉ BRETON

When asked why no reference to love appeared in his two-volume autobiography, Anthony Trollope replied, "If the rustle of a woman's petticoat has ever stirred my blood, of what matter is that to any reader?"

Don't threaten me with love, baby.
                                    BILLIE HOLIDAY

While I have little to say in favor of sex (it's vastly overrated, it's frequently unnecessary, and it's messy), it is greatly to be preferred to the interminable torments of romantic agony through which two people tear one another limb from limb while professing altruistic devotion.   QUENTIN CRISP

A youth with his first cigar makes himself sick—a youth with his first girl makes other people sick.
                                    MARY WILSON LITTLE

The real genius for love lies in not getting into, but getting out of, love.   GEORGE MOORE

When a man has loved a woman, he will do anything for her except continue to love her.
OSCAR WILDE

Thousands have lived without love, not one without water.
W. H. AUDEN

Love: woman's eternal spring and man's eternal fall.
HELEN ROWLAND

There are few people who are not ashamed of their love affairs when the infatuation is over.
LA ROCHEFOUCAULD

Love is not entirely a delirium, yet it has many points in common therewith.
THOMAS CARLYLE

Love is the wisdom of the fool and the folly of the wise.
SAMUEL JOHNSON

True love is like ghosts, which everybody talks about and few have seen.
LA ROCHEFOUCAULD

To say that you can love one person all your life is just like saying that one candle will continue burning as long as you live.
LEO TOLSTOY

The tragedy is not that love doesn't last. The tragedy is the love that lasts.
SHIRLEY HAZZARD

If love be good, from whence cometh my woe?
CHAUCER

The message that "love" will solve all of our problems is repeated incessantly in contemporary culture—like a philosophical tom tom. It would be closer to the truth to say that love is a contagious and virulent disease which leaves a victim in a state of near imbecility, paralysis, profound melancholia, and sometimes culminates in death.

QUENTIN CRISP

It is impossible to love and to be wise.

FRANCIS BACON

Nothing is potent against love save impotence.

SAMUEL BUTLER

Almost all of our relationships begin and most of them continue as forms of mutual exploitation, a mental or physical barter, to be terminated when one or both parties runs out of goods.

W. H. AUDEN

The Book of Life begins with a man and a woman in a garden. It ends with Revelations.

OSCAR WILDE

Love is a hole in the heart. BEN HECHT

[Love] has as few problems as a motorcar. The only problems are the driver, the passengers, and the road. FRANZ KAFKA

No normal man ever fell in love after thirty when the kidneys begin to disintegrate.

H. L. MENCKEN

To fall in love is to create a religion that has a fallible God. JORGE LUIS BORGES

Hoping to fashion a mirror, the lover
doth polish the face of his beloved
until he produces a skull. JOHN UPDIKE

Love is simple to understand if you haven't got a mind soft and full of holes. It's a crutch, that's all, and there isn't any one of us that doesn't need a crutch. NORMAN MAILER

Love's blindness consists oftener in seeing what is not there than in seeing what is.
PETER DE VRIES

The continued propinquity of another human being cramps the style after a time unless that person is somebody you think you love. Then the burden becomes intolerable at once. QUENTIN CRISP

Some women and men seem to need each other.
GLORIA STEINEM

In war as in love, to bring matters to a close, you must get close together. NAPOLEON I

Love will never be ideal until man recovers from
the illusion that he can be just a little bit faithful
or a little bit married. HELEN ROWLAND

I judge how much a man cares for a woman by the space he allots her under a jointly shared umbrella. JIMMY CANNON

Every little girl knows about love. It is only her capacity to suffer because of it that increases.

FRANÇOISE SAGAN

Love is a tyrant sparing none. CORNEILLE

Those who have some means think that the most important thing in the world is love. The poor know that it is money. GERALD BRENAN

Money cannot buy
The fuel of love
but is excellent kindling. W. H. AUDEN

What better proof of love can there be than money? A ten-shilling note shows incontrovertibly just how mad about you a man is. QUENTIN CRISP

Love is mainly an affair of short spasms. If these spasms disappoint us, love dies. It is very seldom that it weathers the experience and becomes friendship. JEAN COCTEAU

The happiest moments in any affair take place after the loved one has learned to accommodate the lover and before the maddening personality of either party has emerged like a jagged rock from the receding tides of lust and curiosity.

QUENTIN CRISP

Falling out of love is very enlightening; for a short while you see the world with new eyes.

IRIS MURDOCH

Fantasy love is much better than reality love. Never doing it is very exciting. The most exciting attractions are between two opposites that never meet.

ANDY WARHOL

The art of love? It's knowing how to join the temperament of a vampire with the discretion of an anemone. E. M. CIORAN

I don't want people to love me. It makes for obligations. JEAN ANOUILH

Love is nothing but a favorable exchange between two people who get the most of what they can expect, considering their value on the personality market. ERICH FROMM

Human love is often but the encounter of two weaknesses. FRANÇOIS MAURIAC

Love is an emotion experienced by the many and enjoyed by the few. GEORGE JEAN NATHAN

What I say is that the supreme and singular joy of making love resides in the certainty of doing evil.

BAUDELAIRE

Tristan and Isolde were lucky to die when they did. They'd have been sick of all that rubbish in a year. ROBERTSON DAVIES

"After she was dead I loved her." That is the story of every life—and death. GORE VIDAL

Love is based on a view of women that is impossible to those who have had any experience with them.   H. L. MENCKEN

To fall in love you have to be in the state of mind for it to take, like a disease.   NANCY MITFORD

There is always something ridiculous about the emotions of people whom one has ceased to love.
                                              OSCAR WILDE

Love is a power too strong to be overcome by anything but flight.   CERVANTES

That desert of loneliness and recrimination that men call love.   SAMUEL BECKETT

Love, for too many men in our time, consists of sleeping with a seductive woman, one who is properly endowed with the right distribution of curves and conveniences and one upon whom a permanent lien has been acquired through the institution of marriage.   ASHLEY MONTAGU

Every love's the love before
In a duller dress.   DOROTHY PARKER

If love is the answer, could you rephrase the question?   LILY TOMLIN

Love is what you feel for a dog or a pussycat. It doesn't apply to humans . . .   JOHNNY ROTTEN

One should always be wary of anyone who promises that their love will last longer than a weekend.
QUENTIN CRISP

If you can stay in love for more than two years, you're *on* something.   FRAN LEBOWITZ

You walk into a room, see a woman, and something happens. It's chemical. What are you going to do about it?
THEODORE DREISER

One is very crazy when in love.   FREUD

❧ GEORGE BERNARD SHAW ❧

GEORGE BERNARD SHAW, the great Anglo-Irish dramatist, critic, and social reformer, was born in Dublin on July 26, 1856. His father was a failed merchant and a drunkard, his mother an indomitable woman who earned money by giving singing lessons. His parents separated and his mother went to London, and at the age of nineteen George followed her there.

During the early London years he wrote five novels as well as art, music, and literary criticism, but he was unable to support himself as a writer. He seldom had pocket money and his clothes were so threadbare that he was ashamed to be seen in public. When his father died and left him a small inheritance, Shaw immediately bought a new suit of clothes.

Shaw spent much of his time in the reading room of the British Museum, where one day he discovered a French translation of Marx's *Das Kapital,* an event that made him a lifelong socialist ("The only book that ever turned me upside down"). He joined the Fabian Society and turned himself into a public speaker, giving hundreds of lectures over the next several years, many of them in support of women's rights.

His zeal to reform British society found ultimate expression in his plays, the first of which, *Widowers' Houses,* was produced in 1892. In the next fifty years he wrote fifty plays, including *Man and Superman, Major Barbara, The Doctor's Dilemma,* and *Pygmalion,* which was the basis of the celebrated musical *My Fair Lady.* Many of the plays were published with long prefaces in which Shaw expressed his views on a wide range of subjects.

With the success of his plays he became a towering public figure with an ego to match (*he* coined the adjective *Shavian*). But there was a marked difference between the overweening GBS and the private Shaw, who confessed to T. E. Lawrence that he had "manufactured" his misanthropic public image, calling it his "greatest work of fiction." Shaw created a persona, what Edmund Wilson called his "comic mask," to hide behind. His famous beard (though originally grown to conceal a smallpox scar) and his trademark Jaeger suit were affectations; he pretended to be an atheist but was deeply religious in his way (he rejected God but embraced "The Life Force"). The real Shaw was painfully shy and sensitive. In private he was kind to children and he answered all his fan mail himself, often enclosing money.

Shaw conducted many epistolary affairs in which he wrote long, adoring letters to various female correspondents ("The perfect love affair is one conducted entirely by post"). But he was naïve and inexperienced with women and remained a virgin until he reached his late twenties ("I had been perfectly continent, except for the involuntary incontinences of dreamland, which were frequent"). He referred to sex as "an irresistible attraction and an overwhelming repugnance and disgust." He fancied himself the reluctant quarry of sexually predaceous women. He wrote to Frank Harris with characteristic immodesty, "As soon as I could afford to dress presentably, I became accustomed to women falling in love with me. I did not pursue women: I was pursued by them."

Among his correspondents was Alice Lockett, a Sunday school teacher who came to his mother's house for singing lessons. Though he wrote her passionate love letters, they probably were not physically intimate. Another of his mother's acquaintances, Jenny Patterson, a well-to-do widow fifteen years his senior, fell hopelessly in love with him. He recorded their affair and his attendant loss of virginity, in his diary: "Had a new experience . . . Seduced and raped." He dropped her when her ardor made him uncomfortable.

When he met May Morris, daughter of the poet William Morris, he was immediately conscious that a "Mystical Betrothal" was "registered in heaven." But he made little or no effort to press the matter, and she eventually lost interest and married someone else.

He corresponded with the actress Ellen Terry for years before they ever met. Although his letters spoke of love, his real interest was in her acting, and he eventually wrote a play for her, *Captain Brassbound's Conversion,* in 1900. They met during rehearsals, and their only physical contact occurred when he kissed her hand. She would write to him of the encounter, "I've seen you at last. You are a boy and a duck."

The list of his liaisons includes many prominent women of the time: the political activist Annie Besant, whom he met when he joined the Fabian Society in 1884; Florence Farr, who played the lead in *Widowers' Houses*; Kate Salt, on whom he would later model *Candida*; Janet Achurch, a married actress, and the artist Bertha Newcombe. Most of these romances were unconsummated. Edith Nesbit, another "conquest," complained bitterly about his lack of passion: "You had no right to write the Preface if you were not going to write the book." If not downright asexual, Shaw was unusually free from the sexual urge. He wrote in the Preface to *Man and Superman,* "The world's books get written, its pictures painted, its statues modelled, its symphonies composed, by people who are free from the otherwise universal dominion of the tyranny of sex."

Shaw met his future wife, Charlotte Payne-Townshend, at a

gathering of Fabians at Beatrice Webb's country house. Though he found her physically uninspiring, he was impressed by her family and her financial independence. They had much to talk about and went cycling and walking together. He wrote her adoring letters ("Ever Dearest . . .").

When Charlotte went to see him at his mother's London house, he was laid up with an infected foot, was obviously in great pain, and looked terrible. She immediately took over his care. She rented a house in the country and took him there to nurse him back to health. He would later tell a biographer, "I never proposed to my wife, you know. It was she who proposed to me and carried me off to marry her." He would also claim that he married her to avoid the scandal of cohabiting without being married. He was forty-one when they married; she was six months his junior. Shaw composed their wedding announcement:

> As a lady and gentleman were out driving in Henrietta st., Covent Garden yesterday, a heavy shower drove them to take shelter in the office of the Superintendent Registrar there, and in the confusion of the moment he married them. The lady was an Irish lady named Miss Payne-Townshend, and the gentleman was George Bernard Shaw. . . .

Charlotte doted on him. She carefully supervised the preparation of his vegetarian meals, did research for and typed many of his plays, and took him all over the world (even though Shaw hated sea travel). But he was difficult. He criticized her relentlessly and deprecated her ideas and opinions so that they quarreled constantly. They often dined in complete silence. Shaw would write in his *Sixteen Self Sketches*, "Not until I was past forty did I earn enough to marry without seeming to marry for money," and that marriage had "ended old gallantries, flirtations and philanderings for both of us." These statements are untrue on all counts: Shaw was indeed interested in her money, marriage did not end at least his postal philandering, and contrary to the innuendo (that marriage had ended philandering for "both" of them), Charlotte was a virgin when they married and probably died a virgin as well.

After he had been married a year Shaw began corresponding with Mrs. Patrick Campbell, "Stella." She was a beautiful and famous actress of thirty-four; he was forty-three and known only as a drama critic. He wrote to her in 1899 to ask her to play the lead in *Caesar and Cleopatra,* which he had written for her. She declined the role, but in the meantime he had fallen in love, and in his subsequent letters he addressed her as "Ever blessedest darling," "Dearest Sillybilly," "Beatricissima," and "Stella Stellarum." She eventually responded in kind, signing her letters with X's at the bottom. She was the love of his life, one of the few of his affairs that was physically consummated.

When Stella announced her intention to marry George Cornwallis West, Shaw fell apart. He begged her to reconsider: "He is young and I am old; so let him wait until I am tired of you." He threatened, pleaded, and cajoled, and when she fled to a seaside hotel he followed her there, but she checked out when he checked in. He finally realized that she meant to go ahead with the wedding, and he resigned himself: "Very well, go. The loss of a woman is not the end of the world. . . . Bah! You have no nerve: you have no brain . . . you know nothing. . . . You have wounded my vanity—an inconceivable audacity, an unpardonable crime. Farewell, wretch that I loved."

Years later, divorced and in need of money, she threatened to publish his letters. He replied angrily:

> Take that terrible wadge of letters, and put it into the hands of any court of honor you can induce your fittest friends to form, or submit it to the judgment of any capable and experienced woman of the world and both will tell you without a moment's hesitation, and with considerable surprise at your having any doubt on the subject, that their public exposure is utterly impossible, except in the physical sense in which it is materially possible for you to undress yourself (or me) in the street.

They traded threats and counterthreats, then, suddenly, Shaw relented and mailed her a check for £4,000, a huge sum at the time. A friend reported that when she opened the envelope and held up the check with trembling hands, there were tears in her eyes. She died a few months later.

❧ Shaw's Garden of Love ❧

Women have been a ghastly nuisance in my life.

All young men greatly exaggerate the difference between one young woman and another.

Woman reduces us all to a common denominator.

It is assumed that the woman must wait, motionless, until she is wooed. That is how the spider waits for the fly.

You sometimes have to answer a woman according to her womanishness, just as you have to answer a fool according to his folly.

Changeable women are more endurable than monotonous ones; they are sometimes murdered but seldom deserted.

I learned more from the first stupid woman who fell in love with me than ever my brains taught me.

The fickleness of the women whom I love is only equalled by the infernal constancy of the women who love me.

———————————

Female murderers get sheaves of offers of marriage.

———————————

Clever and attractive women do not want to vote; they are willing to let men govern as long as they govern men.

———————————

First love is only a little foolishness and a lot of curiosity.

———————————

What I have seen of the love affairs of other people has not led me to regret that deficiency in my experience.

———————————

The whole world is strewn with snares, traps, gins, and pitfalls for the capture of men by women.

———————————

There is never any real sex in romance; what is more, there is very little, and that of a very crude kind, in ninety-nine hundredths of our married life.

It is most unwise for people in love to marry.

A man who desires to get married should know everything or nothing.

A man has no business to marry a woman who can't make him miserable. It means she can't make him happy.

Get married, but never to a man who is home all day.

Marriage is an alliance entered into by a man who can't sleep with the window shut, and a woman who can't sleep with the window open.

What nonsense people talk about happy marriages. A man can be happy so long as he doesn't love her.

A man ought to be able to be fond of his wife without making a fool of himself about her.

MARRIAGE

Marriage is the aftermath of love.

NOEL COWARD

A meal where the soup is better than the dessert.

AUSTIN O'MALLEY

A kind of cosmic, bored familiarity in which everyone watches television, and lives and lets live.

MICHAEL NOVAK

A long conversation chequered by disputes.

ROBERT LOUIS STEVENSON

An honorable agreement among men as to their conduct toward women, and it was devised by women.

DON HEROLD

A sacrament by virtue of which each imparts nothing but vexations to the other.

BALZAC

Rape by contract.

MICHELET

A woman's hair net tangled in a man's spectacles on top of the bedroom dresser.

DON HEROLD

Putting one's hand into a bag of snakes on the chance of drawing out an eel.

LEONARDO DA VINCI

A word which should be pronounced "mirage."

HERBERT SPENCER

Marriage is a bribe to make a housekeeper think she's a householder.

THORNTON WILDER

Marriage is rather a silly habit.   JOHN OSBORNE

Marriage is an adventure, like going to war.
                                   G. K. CHESTERTON

Take it from me, marriage isn't a word—it's a
sentence.   KING VIDOR

Marriage, a market which has nothing free but the
entrance.   MONTAIGNE

I feel sure that no girl could go to the altar, and
would probably *refuse,* if she knew *all* . . .
                                   QUEEN VICTORIA

The Sphinx-riddle. Solve it, or be torn to bits, is
the decree.   D. H. LAWRENCE

A book of which the first chapter is written in
poetry and the remaining chapters in prose.
                                   BEVERLY NICHOLS

Something like the measles; we all have to go
through it.   JEROME K. JEROME

Marrying a man is like buying something you've
been admiring for a long time in a shop window.
You may love it when you get it home, but it
doesn't always go with everything else in the house.
                                   JEAN KERR

I'd marry again if I found a man who had $15
million and would sign over half of it to me before
the marriage, and guarantee he'd be dead within a
year.   BETTE DAVIS

I don't think I'll get married again. I'll just find a woman I don't like and give her a house.

LEWIS GRIZZARD

Should I marry W.? Not if she won't tell me the other letters in her name. And what about her career? How can I ask a woman of her beauty to give up the Roller Derby? Decisions . . .

WOODY ALLEN

❖━━━━━━━━━━━━━━━━━━━━━━━❖

When George IV of England was introduced to his future wife he kissed her hand, recoiled, and whispered to a bystander: "For God's sake, George, give me a glass of brandy!"

❖━━━━━━━━━━━━━━━━━━━━━━━❖

The chief cause of unhappiness in married life is that people think that marriage is sex attraction, which takes the form of promises and hopes and happiness—a view supported by public opinion and by literature. But marriage cannot cause happiness. Instead, it is always torture, which man has to pay for satisfying his sex urge.   TOLSTOY

Passion and marriage are essentially irreconcilable. Their origins and their ends make them mutually exclusive. Their co-existence in our midst constantly raises insoluble problems, and the strife thereby engendered constitutes a persistent danger for every one of our social safeguards.

DENIS DE ROUGEMONT

He married a woman to stop her getting away
Now she's there all day.   PHILIP LARKIN

His designs were strictly honorable, as the phrase
is: that is, to rob a lady of her fortune by way of
marriage.   HENRY FIELDING

Someone once asked me why women don't gamble as much as men do, and I gave the common-sensical reply that we don't have as much money. That was a true but incomplete answer. In fact, women's total instinct for gambling is satisfied by marriage.   GLORIA STEINEM

Marriage . . . is not really a natural state. In nature, coupling is almost always for the sole purpose of mating. Few members of the animal kingdom stay together in couples after mating, except for carrier pigeons and whales. Are you going to stay together with one mate because of carrier pigeons and whales?
DAN GREENBURG AND SUZANNE O'MALLEY

Both in the lower and the middle classes the wiseacres urge young men "to think it over" before taking the decisive step. Thus they foster the delusion that the choice of a wife or husband may be governed by a certain number of accurately weighable pros and cons. This is a crude delusion on the part of common sense.   DENIS DE ROUGEMONT

Spouses are impediments to great enterprises.
SIR FRANCIS BACON

Were a man to consult only his reason, who would marry? For myself, I wouldn't marry, for fear of having a son who resembled me.

NICOLAS CHAMFORT

The only charm of marriage is that it makes a life of deception necessary for both parties.

OSCAR WILDE

By all means marry; if you get a good wife, you'll be happy. If you get a bad one, you'll become a philosopher.

SOCRATES

Never get married while you're going to college; it's hard enough to get a start if a prospective employer finds you've already made one mistake.

KIN HUBBARD

If you are afraid of loneliness, do not marry.

CHEKHOV

A man must marry only a very pretty woman in case he should ever want some other man to take her off his hands.

SACHA GUITRY

No man should marry before he has studied anatomy and dissected the body of a woman.

BALZAC

Only choose in marriage a woman whom you would choose as a friend if she were a man.

JOSEPH JOUBERT

Every woman should marry—and no man.

BENJAMIN DISRAELI

My advice to girls: first, don't smoke—to excess; second, don't drink—to excess; third, don't marry— to excess. MARK TWAIN

People marry for a variety of reasons, and with varying results; but to marry for love is to invite inevitable tragedy. JAMES BRANCH CABELL

A man and a woman marry because both of them do not know what to do with themselves.
CHEKHOV

No woman marries for money; they are all clever enough, before marrying a millionaire, to fall in love with him first. CESARE PAVESE

A man marries to have a home, but also because he doesn't want to be bothered with sex and all that sort of thing. W. SOMERSET MAUGHAM

If they only married when they fell in love, most people would die unwed.
ROBERT LOUIS STEVENSON

Man and wife make one fool. BEN JONSON

He's a fool that marries; but he's a greater fool that does not marry a fool. WILLIAM WYCHERLY

Every man plays the fool once in his life, but to marry is playing the fool all one's life long.
WILLIAM CONGREVE

It's a funny thing that when a man hasn't anything on earth to worry about, he goes off and gets married. ROBERT FROST

Many a marriage hardly differs from prostitution,
except being harder to escape from.
BERTRAND RUSSELL

Strange to say what delight we married people
have to see these poor fools decoyed into our
condition. SAMUEL PEPYS

Marriage is a bargain, and somebody has to get
the worst of the bargain. HELEN ROWLAND

What they do in heaven we are ignorant of; but
what they do not do we are told expressly, they
neither marry nor are given in marriage.
JONATHAN SWIFT

Marriage is neither heaven nor hell; it is simply
purgatory. ABRAHAM LINCOLN

There are some good marriages, but practically no
delightful ones. LA ROCHEFOUCAULD

BARBARA WALTERS: You've been married forty-
two years. What makes your marriage work?
ROBERT MITCHUM: Lack of imagination, I suppose.

If men knew how women pass the time when
they're alone, they'd never marry. O HENRY

I married beneath me—all women do.
NANCY ASTOR

Any intelligent woman who reads the marriage
contract, and then goes into it, deserves all the
consequences. ISADORA DUNCAN

There is nothing in the world like the devotion of
a married woman. It is something no married man
knows anything about.   OSCAR WILDE

What God hath joined together no man shall put
asunder: God will take care of that.
                                    GEORGE BERNARD SHAW

Whom God has put asunder, why should man put
together?   EMERSON

The reason why so few marriages are happy is
because young ladies spend their time making nets,
not in making cages.   JONATHAN SWIFT

Marriage always demands the greatest understanding of the art of insincerity possible between two
human beings.   VICKI BAUM

Politics doesn't make strange bedfellows—marriage
does.   GROUCHO MARX

No compass has ever been invented for the high
seas of matrimony.   HEINRICH HEINE

The critical period in matrimony is breakfast-time.
                                    A. P. HERBERT

It destroys one's nerves to be amiable every day to
the same human being.   BENJAMIN DISRAELI

Marriage must incessantly contend with a monster that devours everything: familiarity.   BALZAC

Most marriages don't add two people together. They subtract one from the other.   IAN FLEMING

Most of the time in married life is taken up by talk.   NIETZSCHE

Marriage is the permanent conversation between two people who talk over everything and everyone until death breaks the record.   CYRIL CONNOLLY

It isn't silence you can cut with a knife any more, it's interchange of ideas. Intelligent discussion of practically everything is what is breaking up modern marriage.   E. B. WHITE

The worst of marriage is that it makes a woman believe that all other men are just as easy to fool.
H. L. MENCKEN

Marriage is hardly a thing one can do now and then, except in America.   OSCAR WILDE

Marriage is the alliance of two people, one of whom never remembers birthdays and the other who never forgets them.   OGDEN NASH

The difficulty with marriage is that we fall in love with a personality, but we must live with a character.
PETER DE VRIES

A man finds himself seven years older the day after
his marriage.   FRANCIS BACON

> During a long and varied career as a bachelor, I
> have noticed that marriage is the death of polite-
> ness between a man and a woman.
>   ARNOLD BENNETT

There are two kinds of marriages: where the husband quotes the wife, and where the wife quotes
the husband.   CLIFFORD ODETS

> When I hear that a friend has fallen into matri-
> mony, I feel the same sorrow as if I had heard of
> his lapsing into theism.   SWINBURNE

A system could not well have been devised more
studiously hostile to human happiness than marriage.
                    PERCY BYSSHE SHELLEY

> Having once embarked on your marital voyage, it
> is impossible not to be aware that you make no
> way and that the sea is not within sight—that, in
> fact, you are exploring an enclosed basin.
>   GEORGE ELIOT

Marriage is traditionally the destiny offered to
women by society. Most women are married or
have been, or plan to be or suffer from not being.
                    SIMONE DE BEAUVOIR

> Marriage is based on the theory that when a man
> discovers a brand of beer exactly to his taste he
> should at once throw up his job and go to work in
> the brewery.   GEORGE JEAN NATHAN

A man in love is incomplete until he is married.
Then he is finished.   ZSA ZSA GABOR

Show me one couple unhappy merely on account
of their limited circumstances, and I will show you
ten who are wretched from other causes.
                    SAMUEL TAYLOR COLERIDGE

Marriage was all a woman's idea, and for man's
acceptance of the pretty yoke it becomes us to be
grateful.   PHYLLIS MCGINLEY

[Marriage] can be compared to a cage: birds outside it despair to enter, and birds within, to escape.
                    MONTAIGNE

If married couples did not live together, happy
marriages would be more frequent.   NIETZSCHE

How marriage ruins a man. It's as demoralizing as
cigarettes, and far more expensive.
                    OSCAR WILDE

Even the God of Calvin never judged anyone as
harshly as married couples judge each other.
                    WILFRID SHEED

It is always incomprehensible to a man that a
woman should refuse an offer of marriage.
                    JANE AUSTEN

Love matches, so called, have illusion for their
father and need for their mother.   NIETZSCHE

Love-matches are made by people who are content, for a month of honey, to condemn themselves to a life of vinegar.

COUNTESS OF BLESSINGTON

Marriage, as practiced by high society, is arranged indecency.   NICOLAS CHAMFORT

When Dorothy Parker married Alan Campbell for the second time she quipped, "People who haven't spoken to each other for years are on speaking terms again today—including the bride and groom."

Squeeze marriage as much as you like, you will never extract anything from it but fun for bachelors and boredom for husbands.   BALZAC

In married life three is company and two is none.

OSCAR WILDE

In our part of the world where monogamy is the rule, to marry means to halve one's rights and double one's duties.   SCHOPENHAUER

We would have broken up except for the children. Who were the children? Well, she and I were.

MORT SAHL

A good marriage would be between a blind wife and a deaf husband.   MONTAIGNE

We sleep in separate rooms, we have dinner apart, we take separate vacations—we're doing everything we can to keep our marriage together.
RODNEY DANGERFIELD

The only thing that holds a marriage together is the husband bein' big enough to step back and see where his wife is wrong.   ARCHIE BUNKER

No man is regular in his attendance at the House of Commons until he is married.
BENJAMIN DISRAELI

In olden times sacrifices were made at the altar—a practice which is still continued.
HELEN ROWLAND

I come from a big family. As a matter of fact, I never got to sleep alone until I was married.
LEWIS GRIZZARD

Marriage is worse than dying. Why stay with *one* person for fifty years? We advise against marriage.
JOEY RAMONE

❧ ORSON BEAN ❧

JW: *How do you define love?*
OB: The best definition I've ever heard is that love is gratitude for shared pleasure, like when my then wife and I would look back and laugh about the funny or outrageous or even terrible things we'd gone through together. One of the disadvantages of not being friends with her now is not being able to pick up the phone

and say, "Hey, there's something on TV about our old neighborhood in Australia." I don't miss having sex with her; I don't even miss her cooking. I miss our being able to laugh together. On second thought, I guess I don't know *what* love is.

JW: *Whatever it is, are Americans any good at it?*

OB: Americans are great risk takers. The French think they have it together because a married Frenchwoman in her fifties can take a lover without having it ruin the marriage. The French chide us: "You Americans all get divorced because you make such a big deal out of infidelity." The French have been doing it the same way for centuries. Americans, on the other hand, are always trying something new. We take chances. And sometimes we fall on our asses. But that's how the human race moves forward.

We did it with our revolution. When the Massachusetts Bay Company passed a law prohibiting the head of a family from killing his recalcitrant son without first getting permission from the elders, everybody screamed, "Godless, atheistic, Communism! The end of the family! If a man can't kill his son, how can he maintain order?" But it was a step forward for civilization.

And when we started the sexual revolution, we moved the race forward in its capacity to handle freedom. On one hand it was inept and foolish and destined to end, but on the other hand it was a tremendous push forward. The French don't take any chances, and therefore they don't learn or grow. They've got it set—the same way their language and their architecture is set.

JW: *Does marriage kill sexual desire?*

OB: I don't know. After the first seven years of our marriage the passion was beginning to wane and I was so greedy to "have it all" that I managed to whip it up by interjecting the idea of our having an open relationship. It provided a second seven years of tremendous passion, but then the marriage just ended, the candle having been burned at both ends.

There's a story about President and Mrs. Coolidge visiting a poultry show. The guide says to Mrs. Coolidge, "You know, ma'am, the rooster here performs his services up to eight or nine times a day," to which the First Lady replied, "Please see to it that the President is given that information!"

A while later the President's party came through the same exhibit and the guide told him, "Sir, Mrs. Coolidge said to be sure to tell you that the rooster there performs his services up to eight or nine times a day."

Coolidge thought for a moment and asked, "Same chicken each time?"

"No, Mr. President, different chickens each time."

"Then see to it that Mrs. Coolidge is given *that* information!"

JW: *Do you read books on how to have a better "relationship"?*

OB: I *used* to read that crap and I spent a lot of time on my marriage, on the *relationship*. I read so many books, I don't know how I had time to take a dump. The men that write these books are really selling out their gender. And the dames who write them are troublemakers, shit stirrers. *Women Who Love Too Much*—all that crap—it's totally irrelevant.

JW: *How are men and women different?*

OB: Men and women are *extremely* different. I've raised two sons and two daughters. We gave the girls hammers and the boys dolls—we went through all that stuff—and it didn't make the least bit of difference. At the age of six our daughters were dressing up like Turkish whores and the boys were out riding their tricycles as fast as they could and trying to get into trouble.

The big difference between men and women is that men are youth and beauty fuckers and women are power fuckers. That goes back to the cave days, and maybe even *before* the cave days, when we were still in the oceans. Jack and Jackie Kennedy are a perfect example, the quintessential couple. After he was killed, she went on to find another kind of power to fuck in Aristotle Onassis. She went from the handsomest and most powerful man in the world to the richest man in the world. For his part, Onassis wanted her because she was the most desirable woman in the world—she had proven it by being Jack Kennedy's wife. He liked doing business with an old, established firm.

There's a *tremendous* difference between the two sexes. We're the same species, but the way we think is so wildly different that we will *never* understand each other, and the best thing we can do is agree to let that be okay.

ORSON BEAN is an actor/writer. His autobiography is entitled *Too Much Is Not Enough*.

☙ MEN ❧

Men are genetically inferior to women.
ANDREA LYNNE

There was, I think, never any reason to believe in any innate superiority of the male, except in his superior muscle.
BERTRAND RUSSELL

Think what cowards men would be if they had to bear children. Women are altogether a superior species.
GEORGE BERNARD SHAW

Most men do not mature, they simply grow taller.
LEO ROSTEN

Men are but children, too, though they have gray hairs; they are only of a larger size.
SENECA

I refuse to consign the whole male sex to the nursery. I insist on believing that some men are my equals.
BRIGID BROPHY

Men are too emotional to vote. Their conduct at baseball games and political conventions shows this, while their innate tendency to appeal to force renders them particularly unfit for the task of government. . . . Man's place is in the armory.
ALICE DUER MILLER

Men are beasts and even beasts don't behave as they do.
BRIGITTE BARDOT

Unusually low voices; short life expectancies; odd, drab costumes; a tendency to sweat, fart and yell.

C. E. CRIMMINS

In all systems of theology the devil figures as a male person.   DON MARQUIS

The more I see of men, the more I like dogs.

MADAME DE STAËL

He'll swim a river of snot, wade nostril deep through a mile of vomit, if he thinks there'll be a friendly pussy waiting for him. He'll screw a woman he despises, any snaggle-toothed hag, and further, pay for the opportunity. And he'll also screw babies and corpses.   VALERIE SOLANAS

A man in the house is worth two in the street.

MAE WEST

Giving a man space is like giving a dog a computer: The chances are he will not use it wisely.

BETTE-JANE RAPHAEL

It isn't the sissy men who help women most, but the rough, capable ones who can be caught and trained.   ED HOWE

Man is a natural polygamist: he always has one woman leading him by the nose, and another hanging on to his coattails.   H. L. MENCKEN

A man's heart may have a secret sanctuary where
only one woman may enter, but it is full of little
anterooms which are seldom vacant.

HELEN ROWLAND

The average man is more interested in a woman
who is interested in him than he is in a woman
with beautiful legs.   MARLENE DIETRICH

Whenever a man encounters a woman in a mood
he doesn't understand, he wants to know if she is
tired.   GEORGE JEAN NATHAN

Passion makes idiots of the cleverest men, and
makes the biggest idiots clever.

LA ROCHEFOUCAULD

Man that is born of woman is apt to be as vain as
his mother.   ROBERT FROST

When every unkind word about women has been
said, we still have to admit, with Byron, that they
are nicer than men. They are more devoted, more
unselfish, and more emotionally sincere. When the
long fuse of cruelty, deceit and revenge is set
alight, it is male thoughtlessness which has fired
it.   CYRIL CONNOLLY

When you see what some girls marry, you realize
how they must hate to work for a living.

HELEN ROWLAND

It's not the men in my life that counts—it's the life in my men. MAE WEST

I love men like some people like good food or wine. GERMAINE GREER

I require three things in a man: he must be handsome, ruthless, and stupid. DOROTHY PARKER

Modern man isn't as virile as he used to be. Instead of making things happen, he waits for things to happen to him. He goes with the current. Something . . . has led him to stop swimming upstream.
MARCELLO MASTROIANNI

Women think of being a man as a gift. It is a duty. Even making love can be a duty. Man has always got to get it up and love isn't always enough.
NORMAN MAILER

He is proud that he has the biggest brain of all the primates, but attempts to conceal that he also has the biggest penis. DESMOND MORRIS

The penis is obviously going the way of the veriform appendix. JILL JOHNSTON

A woman who can't forgive should never have more than a nodding acquaintance with a man.
ED HOWE

Give a man a free hand and he'll run it all over you.   MAE WEST

Man is for woman a means: the end is always the child.   NIETZSCHE

Every man is made of clay and daimon, and no woman can nourish both.   LAWRENCE DURRELL

None of you [men] ask for anything—except everything, but just for so long as you need it.
                                          DORIS LESSING

Men are the reason that women hate one another.
                                          LA BRUYÈRE

Men are those creatures with two legs and eight hands.   JAYNE MANSFIELD

When it comes to women, modern men are idiots. They don't know what they want, and so they never want, permanently, what they get. They want a cream cake that is at the same time ham and eggs and at the same time porridge. They are fools. If only women weren't bound by fate to play up to them.   D. H. LAWRENCE

Men have a much better time of it than women; for one thing they marry later; for another thing they die earlier.   H. L. MENCKEN

I'd never seen men hold each other. I thought the only thing they were allowed to do was shake hands or fight.   RITA MAE BROWN

The male is a domestic animal which, if treated with firmness and kindness, can be trained to do most things.   JILLY COOPER

I only like two kinds of men: domestic and imported.   MAE WEST

Probably the only place where a man can feel really secure is in a maximum security prison, except for the imminent threat of release.   GERMAINE GREER

The first time you buy a house you see how pretty the paint is and buy it. The second time you look to see if the basement has termites. It's the same with men.   LUPE VELEZ

Behind almost every woman you ever heard of stands a man who let her down.   NAOMI BLIVEN

I want a man who's kind and understanding. Is that too much to ask of a millionaire?   ZSA ZSA GABOR

Where's the man could ease a heart
Like a satin gown?   DOROTHY PARKER

Don't accept rides from strange men—and remember that all men are as strange as hell.

ROBIN MORGAN

Men have been trained and conditioned by women, not unlike the way Pavlov conditioned his dogs, into becoming their slaves. As compensation for their labors men are given periodic use of women's vaginas.

ESTHER VILAR

Once you know what women are like, men get kind of boring. I'm not trying to put them down, I mean I like them sometimes as people, but sexually they're dull.

RITA MAE BROWN

The male sex, as a sex, does not universally appeal to me. I find the men today less manly; but a woman of my age is not in a position to know exactly how manly they are.

KATHARINE HEPBURN

To a smart girl men are no problem—they're the answer.

ZSA ZSA GABOR

The men who really wield, retain, and covet power are the kind who answer bedside phones while making love.

NICHOLAS PILEGGI

I am a woman meant for a man, but I never met a man who could compete.

BETTE DAVIS

No man is a hero to his wife's psychiatrist.

ERIC BERNE

You know the problem with men? After the birth, we're irrelevant. DUSTIN HOFFMAN

Plain women know more about men than beautiful ones do. KATHARINE HEPBURN

Macho does not prove mucho. ZSA ZSA GABOR

HS: I have bad news for you: I'm very happily in love. We're entering our sixth month.

JW: *You're at the obnoxious stage?*

HS: Absolutely. I'm afraid I won't be able to give you what you want.

JW: *That's disappointing. But how about a definition of love, anyway?*
HS: It's the only human relationship in which, if a person is seen to be exploited, it can fairly be said they're asking for it.

JW: *How has being in show business affected your love life?*
HS: Not to put too much of a Garrison Keillor gloss on it, but shy guys tend to go into show business because, if they achieve even a modicum of celebrity, the women start doing the difficult work for them. Every day is Sadie Hawkins Day.

JW: *Are Americans any more naïve or clumsy about love or sex than Europeans?*
HS: Yes, because deep down there's something in our culture— the Puritan thing or something—that makes us regret that we have to reproduce this way.

JW: *Is it squeamishness about the act itself?*
HS: I think the Puritans give us the feeling that it's a bad thing, and yet we know it's a good thing. And unlike money, which we feel *and* know is a good thing, we have conflicting emotions about sex. And the conflict makes for clumsiness and awkwardness.

I think we're approaching a time when serial monogamy will be the relationship style-of-choice, which necessarily means having periods of your life when you're dating again at a time when you thought you'd be taking a cruise with some white-haired woman that you've known for forty years, but instead you're *dating* again. America will be full of forty-year-olds saying, "I thought I'd be through with this when I left high school." Dating for life.

JW: *What will happen to the institution of marriage?*
HS: Marriage ceased being a good deal for all concerned as soon

as society made it permissible for women to have sex outside of it. If loan sharks charge three percent annual interest, why go to a bank? Loan sharks are more conveniently located, they have more convenient hours, and their attitudes are better. The only thing that makes them difficult to deal with is the high cost of entry and exit—which is also true of marriage. As much as people like Marvin Mitchelson may try to prolong the social usefulness of marriage by making living together almost as costly, it will ultimately prove to be just a holding action. I have arguments about this with an old girlfriend all the time: the act of getting married, stripped of the necessity to have a secure setting to raise children, seems to me no less grim than registering your emotions with the government.

JW: *Have you ever been married?*

HS: Yes, once, but I had a very good reason: I was making almost no money at the time and my lover was diagnosed with what might have been emphysema, and I wanted to get her covered by my Screen Actors Guild Blue Cross.

JW: *Very romantic.*

HS: If you think that's romantic, we got married in Las Vegas. A Vegas wedding strips the act of getting married of all the extraneous stuff; it's all business. They try to inject a little romance into it, but when you're getting married at four in the morning and you see them slip the organ music cassette into the tape player, some of the majesty is removed. I still have the Visa receipt: "Wedding: $45.00." Aside from giving children a real last name,

I've yet to find a use for marriage. Aside from fueling the alimony industry.

JW: *Are marriage and romantic love incompatible?*

HS: Romantic love is at odds with marriage. Romantic love is probably a transitional stage on the way to wherever it's headed—asexuality if the AIDS virus has its way. It's only recently that we've managed to get free of the arranged marriage for mutual financial advantage to the families; brides in India are still being killed if their dowries aren't up to snuff. It puts marriage in perspective.

JW: *Can you comment on these relationship books such as* Women Who Love Too Much . . .?

HS: *Women Who Love Men Who Hate Women Who Love Men Too Much But Love Men* and on and on. You have to feel sorry for the women who buy this stuff and believe it. Even under the best of circumstances men are hard creatures to trap. Women who flatter themselves into thinking they've trapped one are like people who believe they can get rid of the cockroaches in their kitchen. They're in for a big surprise late one night when they turn on the light.

JW: *Are women more victimized by these books than men?*

HS: Yes. Men are victimized monetarily, but women are victimized by having their whole belief structure shattered. You can always make money, but belief structures are hard to come by.

JW: *What do women want?*

HS: It's easier to answer what men want: Men want great sex and total freedom. I can't generalize about what women want because

I've just run into a woman how defies all my preconceptions I've had the delightful surprise of running into my first non-neurotic, and it's changed my thinking. It makes we want to be fairer than I'd otherwise be in answering the question. I *would* have said that women just want to make men as unhappy as possible, as slowly as possible.

You generalize on the basis of your own experience. Neurotic women, whom bright men tend to gravitate to, have these self-destructive tendencies, and they want to drag you along with them. It took to me a long time to recognize that. It took me a long time to figure out that if you don't want to put up with something, you don't have to. Given sufficient time and patience, it's possible to find someone who meets all your criteria and doesn't make you have to say, "Oh, it's okay, she's just . . ." That sentence is a symptom of the biggest trap of all "Oh, it's okay, she's just . . . It's okay, she's just a little possessive. It's okay, she's just a little unhappy when we have to be separated for a while. It's okay, she's just a little jealous of my coworkers." If you find yourself saying that, you're in the wrong place. On the other hand, how can you pooh-pooh the idea of love if it means being with someone who makes you feel most yourself?

JW: *Why do you think bright men are attracted to neurotic women?*
HS: Bright men are attracted to bright women, and most bright women are neurotic. They've been brought up in a culture that still thinks a bright woman is a bit of an oxymoron and that it can be cured by being fucked enough. *Bright Men Who Love Neurotic*

Women Too Much. I think bright women are challenged to evolve a fairly sly survival strategy early on, and very often, especially if they're attractive, it involves hiding their intelligence. And if they're not absolute eyepoppers, it involves retreating into it. But either way it can twist them.

JW: *What about the impact of feminism?*

HS: Like any good idea, feminism soon became kidnapped by the militants and the crazies—the bra burners—the same way the civil-rights movement turned into "burn whitey" for a while in the late sixties. Now you have the sad spectacle of the only men who responded intellectually to feminism being characterized as softies sitting around in consciousness-raising groups talking about being sensitive.

JW: *Does Shere Hite tick you off?*

HS: I haven't read her book but I've seen her on television. She doesn't tick me off nearly as much as Toni Grant. I mean, to take seriously anything said about relationships by a woman who used to go with Frank Sinatra, Jr., is a big mistake. Not that he isn't a fine singer in his own right.

JW: *But getting back to feminism . . .*

HS: If you've kept your innate sexuality intact, you won't need to buy it back by getting a sexy car; if you've kept your innate femininity intact in the first place, you won't need to demonstrate for it by burning your bra.

I've always thought that the two most restrictive forces were religious rituals and sex-role stereotypes. One was real easy to get free of—I just stopped going to temple. The other was a lot trickier because it involves other people's expectations. Look, feminism is one half of a good idea, the other half being whatever "masculinism" is. Why don't we *all* break free of this jazz?

HARRY SHEARER is an actor/writer and the host of *Le Show* on National Public Radio.

⪻ MY ALL-TIME WORST DATE ⪼

My all-time worst was a girl I took out on a small sailing boat. I had an expensive camera, and after I'd failed to seduce her in the boat and we finally came back to the dock, she dropped the camera into the water. I lost in all directions.
PAUL FUSSELL

When I was in college I was going out with a girl I really wanted to impress. We went to a movie. It was crowded but we saw two seats in the middle of the theater so we started walking sideways the way you do to get to your seat. She was ahead of me and as we were sliding our way down the aisle when I looked down and noticed that my fly was open. So with my right hand, I started to nonchalantly zip it up, but as I did it caught the hair of the girl in the seat in front of me in the zipper. When I pulled up on it her head jerked back violently and she shrieked. It was obviously very painful, it took a long time to extricate her hair from my fly, and it caused a tremendous commotion in the theater.
HOWARD ROSENBERG

I was twenty-two and working at the California State Legislature in Sacramento. I made the youthful mistake of signing up for a computer dating service, and the first person the computer spewed out was someone in San Francisco. On the drive down I built up all sorts of expectations: "Obviously if the computer has gone all this distance to find me somebody, she must be terrific!" Well, when I finally got to her door and she appeared, the woman had a harelip!

Talk about being on your best behavior: first of all, you have a whole new set of problems with where to look. You don't want to look where you *want* to look, and you can't look her in the eye. I'm usually a

---

very slow eater, but I dined with a certain briskness that evening and encouraged her to do likewise. I felt guilty about my reaction to her, but it didn't prevent me from being somewhat abrupt. HARRY SHEARER

Anything my mother had anything to do with goes in the "worst" category. But the very worst was when my sister was at the University of Wisconsin and I was a teenager and my girlfriend and I came to visit her for the weekend and she fixed us up with two of her discards, in my case a very tall gentleman named "Moose." ALICE KAHN

Three-hundred-pound whore in Philadelphia. She broke my bed. It was my first sexual encounter and probably her last. CHARLES BUKOWSKI

He was a *very* attractive man. When he arrived at my house to pick me up, he said there was something wrong with his car so could we possibly use mine? Sure. He drove. We were on a toll road, and he only *pretended* to throw money into the toll machine! And when the alarm went off he remarked that only a *sucker* would put money into a toll machine.

Now, *he* had asked *me* out to dinner, but when we were ordering he looked over the top of his menu and said, "Are you in any position to buy me dinner?" What could I say? Sure. It was an expensive restaurant, but I bought the dinner.

Then he wanted to show me where he lived. It was a beautiful house, but it was pitch black inside. He lit a fire in the fireplace, which cast a little light. He bragged that he had stolen the wood from his former brother-in-law. I was thinking to myself, This guy is crazy, I've got to get out of here. When I asked him where the bathroom was, he gestured vaguely toward a hallway and said, "Oh, it's out there."

It was so dark I could barely see where I was going, but I groped my way to the bathroom and turned the light on, then left it on so I could find my way back to the living room. When I got there he said, "What's the matter with you, I don't own any stock in the electric company!"

It was one of the worst evenings of my life, but the kicker was, I went out with him again! As I said, he was a very attractive guy. I just couldn't believe he could be that bad. I thought maybe he was just having a bad night.

On the second date, I paid for dinner again, he got into a fight with the waiter, who invited him to step outside, but fortunately the maître d' intervened. We went back to my place and in ten minutes he managed to relieve me of a very expensive coffee table book and a favorite record album. I knew I'd never see them again but I didn't care, I just wanted to get rid of him. I couldn't believe the guy. But he *was* awfully attractive.

DIANE WHITE

I am at a loss to understand this question. So far as I know dates are small, sticky fruits which come in a strangely shaped box at Christmas. They are much of a muchness and I can't remember the worst I've had or the best.

HORACE RUMPOLE (JOHN MORTIMER)

When I was twenty-one I thought I was a young man of poise and elegance. I met a beautiful girl and thought she was the dream of my life. I took her to an expensive bar, and when I asked her what she wanted to drink, she demurred. I said I was going to have a Chivas Regal, and she said, "I will too—with Dr Pepper." We ran out of conversation after that and I never called her again.

TAD SZULC

I worked in a small ad agency in Los Angeles with a very lovely, very sexy older woman. We went to dinner. In those days I thought the more liquor you got into a woman the better chance you had of getting somewhere (I had just recently lost my virginity—she was going to be number two). At dinner she must have put away a quart of hard liquor—enough, I thought, to do the trick. I got her into bed and she undressed me, which I thought was pretty far out. Then she went down on me, my first experience of such. I watched in stupefied silence as she drew my member into her mouth . . . and then instantly coughed it and her entire dinner out onto my outraged bare belly. What a turn-on *that* was.

DAN GREENBURG

I went to school in the late sixties. We didn't go on dates; we just sort of hung out listening to records and eventually went to bed—or not, usually not—so I didn't have an all-time worst date. But here's my all-time worst sexual experience: I had just broken up with my girlfriend and the girl had just broken up with her boyfriend, so we decided to have a little fling. We went to bed, and it was okay. It was, like, December. I woke up in the middle of the night in her room, disoriented, and she was the first thing my eyes focused on. She was sitting by the window, staring out, like *Tammy*. I asked her what she was doing and she said, "Oh, nothing, just watching the snow fall. I love you." My stomach turned. You could see my smoke. I never talked to her again.

IAN SHOALES

I let a guy pick me up at a bus stop when I was fifteen. I talked my mother into letting me have a date with him. He turned into a real creep intent on date rape. Then he desisted and made fun of my naïveté, I sure was glad to get home and pretend to my mother that she hadn't been right to worry.

LIZ SMITH

The year was 1947, her name was Jacqueline Bouvier, and she was at Vassar and I was at Williams College. A fraternity brother had invited her to a weekend Williams house party but, at the last minute, he was stricken with mononucleosis and asked me to meet Jackie at the train from Poughkeepsie and pinch-hit for him. Meeting me for the first time, she was clearly displeased with the substitution. Nor was this a girl who was accustomed to blind dates. She was already sort of famous, having had her picture in *Life* as one of the year's top debutantes. Though I was a writer for the college magazine, I was not exactly a Big Man on Campus, nor was I in a position to introduce her to the Adonises who *were* the B.M.O.C.'s, such as the athletic team captains, the class president, etc., all of whom she'd come expecting to meet. My sick friend remained in the infirmary all weekend, and I was saddled with a sorely disappointed young lady the whole time. I did my best, but it was uphill all the way. Interestingly, when I have encountered the lady over the years and have mentioned that weekend, she claims to have no recollection of it whatsoever.   STEPHEN BIRMINGHAM

I have two all-time worst dates. One was with an Iranian gentleman who was very nice but who spoke little English and was an insane driver. He drove me up to Big Bear, rowed me out into the middle of a lake and suggested that we make love. Since neither one of us could swim, and since he could barely row, I simply declined his offer and that was that.

The other date was just a really dumb, ordinary date in college with a guy that I'd known for a long time. I don't know if this still happens, but back in the old days guys would turn during the last fifteen minutes of any given date into some kind of insane gorilla. I'd known him as a friend for years but this was our first date and he changed from a nice boy into a demented gorilla. When I nimbly jumped out of the car, he knocked out a tooth! He's now a very famous surgeon in town, so I can't give his name. But whenever I see him I say, "Hi, remember our really terrible date?" and he says, "Carolyn, you must be mistaken, that wasn't me, I could never do that." And I'm sure he believes it.   CAROLYN SEE

In adolescence I had nothing but worst dates. I guess the worst was a freshman "mixer" at Cornell where *nobody* asked me to dance. I ran away.
EDA LE SHAN

It was with a guy whom I liked as a person but whom I did not want to be my boyfriend. We had been dating for a while but I couldn't stand him anymore. It was agonizing to go out on the last date, at the end of which I knew I would have to tell him it was over. I can remember sitting in the movie theater and cringing because he was holding my hand: I did not *want* this guy holding my hand. I tried to imagine that my whole arm didn't belong to me, tried to disconnect myself from my arm. It was an excruciating evening, and the longest movie I've ever seen.   MAGGIE SCARF

It was recently. I had a date with a rich old guy who owns a paper factory in Pennsylvania. Before we left my house he called the factory to see what was going on. At dinner instead of de-caf or coffee he ordered hot water. Then he excused himself and checked the factory again.

On the way home he got lost and had to go into a filling station for directions. He left the car in gear and it rolled into a police car. The cops wanted to give *me* a ticket because I was alone in the car! I explained that I was only trying to stop it but couldn't do it in time because my sleeve got caught on the gear shift and I couldn't find the brake.

When we got back to my house my date made another call to the paper factory. I bid him a very cordial good night because I knew I would never, *ever* see him again.   PHYLLIS DILLER

I had lusted after Dora for years. We dated in a time when nice girls didn't go all the way, so we didn't, but several times there we went 97% of the way. She married another. Years pass. I see her infrequently with the simple-minded asshole she chose over an obviously superior person. My lust continues. More years pass. Then I am in her city and learn she has been divorced by her husband. (Didn't I tell you he was a simple-minded asshole?) I call "their" home and cleverly ask for her former husband, expressing astonishment when she tells me the marriage has gone kaput. Ever-so-casually I ask her out for dinner.

I bathe, powder, deodorize, dress in my best, walk the hotel lobby looking at my watch every ten seconds, alternately growling away old friends who want to chat and thanking sweet Jesus for my chance at Dora. A hump-backed old dowager approaches, carrying one of the books I have authored. I unsling my trusty pen, bark, "I'm-meeting-somebody-and-I'm-in-a-hurry-how-do-you-want-this-signed?" And the bent old crone says, "How about, 'Love and kisses to Dora'?" Things went downhill from there.   LARRY L. KING

I have had very few dates other than with the two women I married and they were all pleasant dates. No exceptions. I make them so.

ISAAC ASIMOV

I took a gentleman on a beautiful trail ride. He wasn't a good rider so I put him on the safest, slowest horse in the barn. As luck would have it his horse stepped in a hornet's nest. After that episode in which his horse ran faster than Secretariat, ardor hit the deep freeze. My second worst date occurred when a quite pretty lady asked me out and I was thrilled that she had noticed me. I met her at the appointed time at a posh restaurant only to be greeted by her and her husband. I was both naïve and shocked.   RITA MAE BROWN

I had a date with somebody and she sent her roommate in her place. It gave me an insight into how women feel when they're treated as objects. I felt like I was being passed from one to another just because I was a good lay. An easy one. The word was out. "Does he put out?" "Yeah."
                                                                PAUL KRASSNER

Time has mercifully obliterated the details of my worst date. But I can recall one or two wasted evenings with men who spent three hours discussing the very young women they were thinking of breaking up with. An hour seemed an eternity with the cardiologist who chainsmoked.
                                                                GAEL GREENE

His name was Roger. We had nothing in common; we were together seven years. He was married. I don't want to talk about it. Let me say this: I've been dating for almost 20 years. And, as bad as many dates have been—if experience teaches anything— it's that things will only get worse. So, I would have to conclude that my very worst date is yet to come.   LINDA SUNSHINE

None of your business.   URSULA K. LE GUIN

The story of the Duke and Duchess of Windsor is the saddest love story ever told, sadder than *Romeo and Juliet*, *Antony and Cleopatra*, and *Tristan and Isolde* combined. The Duke did what many yearn to do: he chucked it all for love. And in doing so, he exposed the truth about romantic love.

On the surface it seemed glorious, the stuff that dreams—or at least a miniseries, a Masterpiece Theatre production, and countless books and articles—are made of. But beneath the surface, it was less *Romeo and Juliet* than *Comedy of Errors,* a classic case of mistaken identity. She fell in love with a monarch; he was looking for someone to rule him. She wanted to be mistress to a king but ended up wife to an exile. He wanted a dutiful wife and a cottage in the country but ended up in a hotel with a woman who lived to shop and loved to rumba.

If love means never having to see your lover as he or she really is, marriage is a rude eye-opener. By the time the Windsors were married it was too late: They were locked into an ideal as brittle as the plastic figures on a wedding cake. Their life together was an aimless round of nightclubs, dinner parties, and fashion shows.

Wallis once complained that unlike other couples, they could never be "ordinary." But that's just the point: They weren't ordinary, they were myth made flesh, the paradigm of romantic love. Yet the café-society photographs taken during their long, hollow marriage tell another story: The Duchess, needle-thin, her taut face a vapid mask; the Duke, wearing a party hat and an embarrassed smile amid balloons and banners. Born to be a king, he lived—and died—a jester.

Beholding the Love Story of the Century is a little like looking at Gestalt drawings: Is it a lamp or is it a lady? Did he abdicate for the woman he loved, or did he fall in love so he could abdicate? After all, the not very young, not very pretty, twice-divorced American adventuress was the perfect choice for a man determined to denounce his patrimony. Ironically, the Windsors *do* epitomize romantic love: Their relationship was empty, irresponsible, and founded on delusion.

໑ SEX ໖

Sex is God's joke on human beings. BETTE DAVIS

Sex is work.   ANDY WARHOL

The last refuge of the miserable. QUENTIN CRISP

Sex is a pleasurable exercise in plumbing, but be
careful or you'll get yeast in your drain tap.
RITA MAE BROWN

The sexual drive is nothing but the motor memory
of previously remembered pleasure.
WILHELM REICH

We tried it twice and it worked both times.
ROBERT BENCHLEY, on sex with Mrs. Benchley
(the Benchleys had two children)

Social confusion has now reached a point at which
the pursuit of immorality turns out to be more
exhausting than compliance with the old moral
codes.   DENIS DE ROUGEMONT

According to the latest research, 60% of American
couples are now screwing dog fashion—so both
parties can watch television in bed.
BILLY WILDER

Maybe I'll make a "Mary Poppins" movie and
shove the umbrella up my ass.

MARILYN CHAMBERS

In the case of some women, orgasms take quite a
bit of time. Before signing on with such a partner,
make sure you are willing to lay aside, say, the
month of June, with sandwiches having to be
brought in.   BRUCE JAY FRIEDMAN

Man survives earthquakes, epidemics, the horrors
of disease, and all the agonies of the soul, but for
all time his tormenting tragedy is, and will be, the
tragedy of the bedroom.   TOLSTOY

❖━━━━━━━━━━━━━━━━━━━━━━━━❖

After participating in an orgy and being invited back the very next night,
Voltaire declined with the following explanation: "Once, a philosopher;
twice, a pervert!"

❖━━━━━━━━━━━━━━━━━━━━━━━━❖

Of all the animals on earth, none is so brutish as
man when he seeks the delirium of coition.

EDWARD DAHLBERG

For the butterfly, mating and propagation involve
the sacrifice of life, for the human being, the sacrifice of beauty.   GOETHE

The ability to make love frivolously is the chief characteristic which distinguishes human beings from beasts.   HEYWOOD BROUN

After coitus every animal is sad, except the human female and the rooster.   GALEN

One night I was sitting with friends at a table in a crowded Key West bar. At a nearby table, there was a mildly drunk woman with a very drunk husband. Presently, the woman approached us and asked me to sign a paper napkin. All this seemed to anger her husband; he staggered over to the table, and after unzipping his trousers and hauling out his equipment, said: "Since you're autographing things, why don't you autograph this?" The tables surrounding us had grown silent, so a great many people heard my reply, which was: "I don't know if I can autograph it, but perhaps I can *initial* it."   TRUMAN CAPOTE

The most exciting attractions are between two opposites that never meet.   ANDY WARHOL

I don't see much of Alfred any more since he got so interested in sex.   MRS. ALFRED KINSEY

There may be some things better than sex, and there may be some things worse. But there's nothing exactly like it.   W. C. FIELDS

No one, thank goodness, advocates that people should go about with long green strands of snot dangling from their noses in the name of nasal freedom, yet quite a few people have been converted in recent years to a belief that it is permissible for them to inflict the sights, sounds and smells of their bodies on any innocent bystander in the name of "sexual freedom."   QUENTIN CRISP

The sexual organs are the most sensitive organs of the human being. The eye or the ear seldom sabotages you. An eye will not stop seeing if it doesn't like what it sees. I would say that the sexual organs express the human soul more than any other limb of the body. They are not diplomats. They tell the truth ruthlessly. It's nice to deal with them and their caprices, but they are even more *meshuga* than the brain.   ISAAC BASHEVIS SINGER

Sexual intercourse is a slight attack of apoplexy.
                DEMOCRITUS

I could be content that we might procreate like trees, without conjunction, or that we were any way to perpetuate the world without this trivial and vulgar way of coition; it is the foolishest act a wise man commits in all his life.
                SIR THOMAS BROWNE

Physiological expenditure is a superficial way of self-expression. People who incline toward physical love accomplish nothing at all.
                SALVADOR DALI

Older women are best because they always think
they may be doing it for the last time.

IAN FLEMING

◆━━━━━━━━━━━━━━━━━━━━━━━━◆

The Hungarian novelist Ferenc Molnar, told that this mistress had been
unfaithful to him while he was out of town: "She sleeps with others
because she loves them, but for *money,* only with me!"

◆━━━━━━━━━━━━━━━━━━━━━━━━◆

"O 'Melia, my dear, this does everything crown!
Who could have supposed I should meet you in town?
And whence such fair garments, such prosperity?"—
"O didn't you know I'd been ruined?" said she.

THOMAS HARDY

The man takes a body that is not his, claims it,
sows his so-called seed, reaps a harvest—he colo-
nizes a female body, robs it of its natural re-
sources, controls it.   ANDREA DWORKIN

Nothing risque, nothing gained.

ALEXANDER WOOLLCOTT

Intercourse is an assertion of mastery, one that
announces his own higher caste and proves it upon
a victim who is expected to surrender, serve, and
be satisfied.   KATE MILLETT

Whoever named it necking was a poor judge of
anatomy.   GROUCHO MARX

It is certainly very hard to write about sex in English without making in unattractive.

EDMUND WILSON

We are not taught to think decently on sex subjects, and consequently we have no language for them except indecent language.

GEORGE BERNARD SHAW

The tragedy is when you've got sex in the head instead of down where it belongs.

D. H. LAWRENCE

I've tried several varieties of sex. The conventional position makes me claustrophobic. And the others give me either a stiff neck or lockjaw.

TALLULAH BANKHEAD

❖━━━━━━━━━━━━━━━━━━━━━━━━━━━❖

When asked if the Prince of Wales was a romantic lover, Lillie Langtry replied, "Oh, not at all—just a straight-away pounder."

❖━━━━━━━━━━━━━━━━━━━━━━━━━━━❖

As for the topsy turvy tangle known as *soixante-neuf,* personally I have always felt it to be madly confusing, like trying to pat your head and rub your stomach at the same time.

HELEN LAWRENSON

Conventional sexual intercourse is like squirting jam into a doughnut.   GERMAINE GREER

My husband is German; every night I get dressed
up like Poland and he invades me.

BETTE MIDLER

There are a number of mechanical devices which
increase sexual arousal, particularly in women.
Chief among these is the Mercedes-Benz 380SL
convertible.   P. J. O'ROURKE

It doesn't matter what you do in the bedroom as
long as you don't do it in the street and frighten
the horses.   MRS. PATRICK CAMPBELL

❖━━━━━━━━━━━━━━━━━━━━━━━━━━━━❖

While touring the United States in 1960, Brendan Behan visited John
Cheever at his rented house in Scarborough, New York. When Behan
came out to the pool for a swim, Cheever's landlady, a Mrs. Vanderlip,
turned out in hopes of meeting the celebrated author of *Borstal Boy*. "I'm
much more interested in farney now that I'm off the sauce," Behan
announced. "What is farney?" asked Mrs. Vanderlip. "Farney, Mam,"
said Behan, "is an abbreviation for farnication."

❖━━━━━━━━━━━━━━━━━━━━━━━━━━━━❖

Sex is not only a divine and beautiful activity; it's
a murderous activity. People kill each other in
bed. Some of the greatest crimes ever committed
were committed in bed. And no weapons were
used.   NORMAN MAILER

The act of procreation and the members employed therein are so repulsive, that if it were not for the beauty of the faces and the adornments of the actors and the pent-up impulse, nature would lose the human species   LEONARDO DA VINCI

The only difference between sex and death is, with death you can do it alone and nobody's going to make fun of you.   WOODY ALLEN

Coition, sometimes called "the little death," is more like a slight attack of apoplexy.

PAULINE SHAPLER

The genitals themselves have not undergone the development of the rest of the human form in the direction of beauty.   SIGMUND FREUD

❖━━━━━━━━━━━━━━━━━━━━━━━━━━━━━❖

Sigmund Freud was an inveterate cigar smoker. When asked by a student whether his cigar smoking was a symbolic activity, Freud replied, "Sometimes a cigar is just a cigar."

❖━━━━━━━━━━━━━━━━━━━━━━━━━━━━━❖

Chastity is sexual intercourse with affection.

ROBERT OWEN

Chastity is curable, if detected early.   ANONYMOUS

Give me chastity, but not yet.   ST. AUGUSTINE

Most plain girls are virtuous because of the scarcity of opportunity to be otherwise.

MAYA ANGELOU

Filth and old age, I'm sure you will agree,
Are powerful wardens upon chastity.   CHAUCER

The advantage of being celibate is that when one sees a pretty girl one does not need to grieve over having an ugly one back home.   PAUL LÉAUTAUD

Nature abhors a virgin—a frozen asset.

CLARE BOOTH LUCE

A man has missed something if he has never woken up in an anonymous bed beside a face he'll never see again, and if he has never left a brothel at dawn feeling like throwing himself into the river out of sheer disgust with life.   FLAUBERT

❖━━━━━━━━━━━━━━━━━━━━━━━━━━❖

The revivalist preacher Father Divine did not always practice what he preached. One of his "private secretaries" caused a scandal when she revealed his seduction technique: "Mary wasn't a virgin," he would whisper.

❖━━━━━━━━━━━━━━━━━━━━━━━━━━❖

I can't understand why more people aren't bisexual. It would double your chances for a date on Saturday night.   WOODY ALLEN

My own belief is that there is hardly anyone whose sexual life, if it were broadcast, would not fill the world at large with surprise and horror.

W. SOMERSET MAUGHAM

The man and woman make love, attain climax, fall separate. Then she whispers, "I'll tell you who I was thinking of if you tell me who you were thinking of." Like most sex jokes the origin of the pleasant exchange are obscure. But whatever the source, it seldom fails to evoke a certain awful recognition.

GORE VIDAL

The big mistake that men make is that when they turn thirteen or fourteen and all of a sudden they've reached puberty, they believe that they like women. Actually, you're just horny. It doesn't mean you like women any more at twenty-one than you did at ten.

JULES FEIFFER

Love is the answer, but while you're waiting for the answer, sex raises some pretty good questions.

WOODY ALLEN

I know nothing about sex, because I was always married.

ZSA ZSA GABOR

Boy meets girl; girl gets boy into pickle; boy gets pickle into girl.

JACK WOODFORD

JW: *What's your definition of romantic love?*
RMB: Romantic love is a willing suspension of disbelief in order

to be entertained. My feeling is that you can enjoy the same experience by attending the theater, with generally better results.

JW: *What are the essential differences between men and women?*

RMB: Their pay scales. That's my attitude. My mother thought that the essential difference between men and women was that men fall in love with their eyes, women with their ears. She had a point there: Men do seem to be more visually driven than women.

JW: *Is the institution of marriage bankrupt?*

RMB: Not if you marry a Rockefeller.

JW: *Are passion and marriage irreconcilable?*

RMB: Yes. Marriage is akin to a corporate merger. One is supposed to look for stability, competence, and steady returns on your investment. Passion is antithetical to those values. Perhaps people need the fleeting emotion of passion to bring them to the quite frightening altar. I mean, when you marry, honey, you are signing on for life in front of God and everybody.

JW: *Do you agree with La Rochefoucauld's remark, "People would never fall in love if they had not heard love talked about"?*

RMB: People would continue to fall in love, but perhaps like in ancient Greece, it would be regarded as a state of diminished sanity. Somewhere along the line, they say the court of Eleanor of Aquitaine (in the twelfth century—but a scholar can dispute that) the concept of romantic love was invented. We've been struggling with it ever since, as did La Rochefoucauld.

JW: *Are portrayals of love on television and in movies accurate?*

RMB: Ha, they aren't bad enough! The real substance of developing a relationship is always interrupted by deodorant commercials.

They save the beer commercials for baseball, or maybe they think beer drinkers aren't interested in love. Could be.

JW: *What do you think of computer dating?*

RMB: It's terrific if you're a computer.

JW: *Are the rich different when it comes to love or sex?*

RMB: No. If anything the rich are the victims of the less rich or non-rich, who fall in love with their bank accounts. No wonder they stick together. If you love another rich person, it probably won't be because of their money—I hope so, anyway. Love is difficult regardless of class, race, sex, sexual preference. It's easier to love the whole human race than one complicated individual.

JW: *Is the sexual revolution over?*

RMB: No. The people who exploded into the sexual revolution are hitting middle age and middle age is hitting back, but the young are out there actively pursuing orgasms and thinking they're immortal. Given the fact that sex can now kill you— slowly—I find this hormonal rage poignant. How can we blame the young for doing what we did ourselves, and yet how can we not warn them because the times are so very different? Unfortunately, too many people think it won't happen to them.

JW: *What are the results of the sexual revolution?*

RMB: A lot of bad novels in which the clitoris is described as the red pearl and the penis is always described as engorged and throbbing. Mercy.

JW: *Is the image of men as uncommunicative an accurate one?*

RMB: No. I've met just as many uncommunicative women as men. To me the difference is in the willingness to look inside, to realize one's own emotions. Often it takes men longer to do that because the culture doesn't support such self-knowledge. So maybe the difference is that the average man, if there is such an animal, communicates less of himself because he knows less of himself than the average woman. I really don't know—but I think that sexually polarizing behavior and expectations is the road to disillusionment, disharmony, and divorce. I mistrust "men and women" questions even as I try to answer them.

JW: *Are women better at love? Sex? Commitment?*

RMB: Well, if our divorce rate is any indication, women aren't any better at love, sex, and commitment than men, because it takes two to tango. Or perhaps the bonds of matrimony are so heavy, it takes two to carry them—sometimes three. There's a good reason for divorce!

RITA MAE BROWN is the author of *Rubyfruit Jungle, Starting from Scratch,* and *Bingo.* She lives in Charlottesville, Virginia.

THE DIFFERENCE BETWEEN MEN AND WOMEN

Where young boys plan for what they will achieve and attain, young girls plan for whom they will achieve and attain.   CHARLOTTE PERKINS GILMAN

Women, as they grow older, rely more and more on cosmetics. Men, as they grow older, rely more and more on a sense of humor.

GEORGE JEAN NATHAN

Strange difference of sex, that time and circumstance, which enlarge the views of most men, narrow the views of women almost invariably.

THOMAS HARDY

Women speak because they wish to speak, whereas a man speaks only when driven to speech by something outside himself—like, for instance, he can't find any clean socks.   JEAN KERR

Women aren't embarrassed when they buy men's pajamas, but a man buying a nightgown acts as though he were dealing with a dope peddler.

JIMMY CANNON

Men marry because they are tired; women marry because they are curious. Both are disappointed.

OSCAR WILDE

A woman's guess is much more accurate than a man's certainty.   RUDYARD KIPLING

It is a woman's business to get married as soon as possible, and a man's to keep unmarried as long as he can.   GEORGE BERNARD SHAW

All men laugh at the Three Stooges and all women think that the Three Stooges are assholes.
                                    JAY LENO

A woman's head is always influenced by her heart, but a man's heart is always influenced by his head.
                                    COUNTESS OF BLESSINGTON

No male can beat a female in the long run because they have it over us in sheer, damn longevity.
                                    JAMES THURBER

Women represent the triumph of matter over mind, just as men represent the triumph of mind over morals.   OSCAR WILDE

A tranquil woman can go on sewing longer than an angry man can go on fuming.
                                    GEORGE BERNARD SHAW

To women, love is an occupation; to men, a preoccupation.   LIONEL STRACHEY

Woman understands children better than man does, but man is more childlike than woman.
                                    NIETZSCHE

Man makes love by braggadocio, and woman makes love by listening.   H. L. MENCKEN

Men are more interesting than women, but women are more fascinating. JAMES THURBER

Of the two lots, the woman's lot of perpetual motherhood, and the man's of perpetual babyhood, I prefer the man's.

GEORGE BERNARD SHAW

Man's objection to love is that it dies hard; woman's, that when it is dead, it stays dead.

H. L. MENCKEN

There are two sides to the story when men quarrel, but at least a dozen when women quarrel.

ED HOWE

God is for men, and religion for women.

JOSEPH CONRAD

Women become attached to men by the intimacies they grant them; men are cured of their love by the same intimacies. LA BRUYÈRE

When he will, she won't; and when he won't, she will. TERENCE

In love women are professionals, men are amateurs.

FRANÇOIS TRUFFAUT

Women prefer to talk in two's, while men prefer to talk in three's. G. K. CHESTERTON

A man keeps another person's secret better than his own, a woman keeps her own better than another's. LA BRUYÈRE

Every time a woman leaves off something she looks better, but every time a man leaves off something he looks worse.　WILL ROGERS

The man's desire is for the woman; the woman's desire is for the desire of the man.　COLERIDGE

Male sexual response is far brisker and more automatic. It is triggered easily by things—like putting a quarter in a vending machine.　ALEX COMFORT

Fighting is essentially a masculine idea; a woman's weapon is her tongue.　HERMIONE GINGOLD

Love is the whole history of a woman's life, but it is an episode in man's.　MADAME DE STAËL

Men are brought up to command, women to seduce.　SALLY KEMPTON

A man says what he knows, a woman says what will please.　JEAN-JACQUES ROUSSEAU

A successful man is one who makes more money than his wife can spend. A successful woman is one who can find such a man.　LANA TURNER

When man and woman die, as poets sung,
His heart's the last part moves, her last, the tongue.
　BENJAMIN FRANKLIN

When a woman marries again it is because she detested her first husband. When a man marries again, it is because he adored his first wife. Women try their luck; men risk theirs. OSCAR WILDE

As vivacity is the gift of women, gravity is that of men. JOSEPH ADDISON

The average woman is at the head of something with which she can do as she likes; the average man has to obey orders and do nothing else.
G. K. CHESTERTON

What is most beautiful in virile men is something feminine; what is most beautiful in feminine women is something masculine. SUSAN SONTAG

The wholly manly man lacks the wit necessary to give objective form to his soaring and secret dreams, and the wholly womanly woman is apt to be too cynical a creature to dream at all.
H. L. MENCKEN

The happiness of man is: I will. The happiness of women is: he wills. NIETZSCHE

In our civilization, men are afraid that they will not be men enough and women are afraid that they might be considered only women.
THEODOR REIK

A man loses his sense of direction after four drinks; a woman loses hers after four kisses.
H. L. MENCKEN

Women eat while they are talking; men talk while
they are eating.   MALCOLM DE CHAZAL

Most women have all other women as adversaries;
most men have all other men as their allies.
GELETT BURGESS

Men live by forgetting—women live on memories.
T. S. ELIOT

Women have a less accurate measure of time than
men: there is a clock in Adam, none in Eve.
EMERSON

If I were asked to describe the difference between
the sexes in the gay world, I would say that the
men wanted to be amused; the girls sought
vindication.   QUENTIN CRISP

Even the wisest men make fools of themselves
about women, and even the most foolish women
are wise about men.   THEODOR REIK

Men at most differ as heaven and earth,
But women, worst and best, as heaven and hell.
ALFRED LORD TENNYSON

Men play the game; women know the score.
ROGER WODDIS

Women are quite unlike men. Women have higher
voices, longer hair, smaller waistlines, daintier feet
and prettier hands. They also invariably have the
upper hand.   STEPHEN POTTER

The word love has by no means the same sense for both sexes, and this is one cause of the serious misunderstandings that divide them.

SIMONE DE BEAUVOIR

It is a mistake for a taciturn, serious-minded woman to marry a jovial man, but not for a serious-minded man to marry a light-hearted woman.

GOETHE

Woman wants monogamy;
Man delights in novelty.
Love is a woman's moon and sun;
Man has other forms of fun.
Woman lives but in her lord;
Count to ten and man is bored.

DOROTHY PARKER

In a husband there is only a man; in a married woman there is a man, a father, a mother, and a woman.

BALZAC

It is probable that both in life and in art the values of a woman are not the values of a man.

VIRGINIA WOOLF

Women are never disarmed by compliments. Men always are. That is the difference between the sexes.

OSCAR WILDE

Woman's dearest delight is to wound man's self-conceit, though man's dearest delight is to gratify hers.

GEORGE BERNARD SHAW

A man must be potent and orgasmic to ensure the future of the race. A woman need only be available.
WILLIAM H. MASTERS AND VIRGINIA E. JOHNSON

Man seems not so much wicked as frail, unable to face pain, trouble and growing old. A good woman knows that nature is her enemy. Look at what it does to her.
FAY WELDON

The ability to have our own way, and at the same time convince others they are having their own way, is a rare thing among men. Among women it is as common as eyebrows.
THOMAS BAILEY ALDRICH

Words are women, deeds are men.
GEORGE HERBERT

A man is as good as he has to be, and a woman as bad as she dares.
ELBERT HUBBARD

A woman's a woman til the day she dies, but a man's a man only as long as he can.
MOMS MABLEY

Women are smarter than men because they listen.
PHIL DONAHUE

Men want to put their signature at the bottom; women don't want to finish that letter.
IAN SHOALES

Male and female are really two cultures and their life experiences are utterly different.
KATE MILLETT

Throughout history, females have picked providers for males. Males pick anything.

MARGARET MEADE

The silliest woman can manage a clever man; but it needs a clever woman to manage a fool.

RUDYARD KIPLING

You see an awful lot of smart guys with dumb women, but you hardly ever see a smart woman with a dumb guy.

ERICA JONG

You never see a man walking down the street with a woman who has a little pot belly and a bald spot.

ELAYNE BOOSLER

Girls got balls. They're just a little higher up, that's all.

JOAN JETT

What women look for in a man: Breathing, IQ over 80, weight under 550 pounds, fewer than six ex-wives. What men look for in a woman: Pia Zadora as she was ten years ago.

C. E. CRIMMINS

❧ WIVES ❧

A man's wife is his compromise with the illusion
of his first sweetheart.   GEORGE JEAN NATHAN

> When wives come in the door, wisdom escapes by
> the window.   SCHOPENHAUER

I am too much interested in other men's wives to
think of getting one of my own.
    GEORGE MOORE

> Everybody all over the world takes a wife's esti-
> mate into account in forming an opinion of a
> man.   BALZAC

He knows little who tells his wife all he knows.
    THOMAS FULLER

> A loving wife will do anything for her husband
> except stop criticizing him and trying to improve
> him.   J. B. PRIESTLEY

Ne'er take a wife till thou hast a house (and a fire)
to put her in.   BENJAMIN FRANKLIN

> She has buried all her female friends; I wish she
> would make friends with my wife.   MARTIAL

Since all the maids are good and lovable, from
whence come the bad wives?   CHARLES LAMB

My wife's idea of roughing it is staying at a Holiday Inn with single-ply toilet paper.   ABBY DAN

The man who enters his wife's dressing room is either a philosopher or a fool.   BALZAC

The woman who cannot tell a lie in defense of her husband, is unworthy of the name of wife.
ELBERT HUBBARD

He that displays too often his wife and his wallet is in danger of having both of them borrowed.
BENJAMIN FRANKLIN

The best way of revenging yourself on a man who has stolen your wife is to leave her to him.
SACHA GUITRY

Wives are people who feel they don't dance enough.
GROUCHO MARX

A good wife is good, but the best wife is not so good as no wife at all.   THOMAS HARDY

A man's wife has more power over him than the state has.   EMERSON

An ideal wife is one who remains faithful to you but tries to be just as charming as if she weren't.
SACHA GUITRY

A man's mother is his misfortune, but his wife is his fault.   WALTER BAGEHOT

My wife doesn't care what I do when I'm away, as long as I don't have a good time.   LEE TREVINO

A sweetheart is a bottle of wine, a wife is a wine bottle.   BAUDELAIRE

Each [of my wives] was jealous and resentful of my preoccupation with business. Yet none showed any visible aversion to sharing in the proceeds.
                                                J. PAUL GETTY

There is no fury like an ex-wife searching for a new lover.   CYRIL CONNOLLY

A husband should not insult his wife publicly, at parties. He should insult her in the privacy of the home.   JAMES THURBER

I'm having trouble managing the mansion. What I need is a wife.   ELLA T. GRASSO

Basically my wife was immature. I'd be at home in the bath and she'd come in and sink my boats.
                                                WOODY ALLEN

The trouble with my wife is that she is a whore in the kitchen and a cook in bed.
                                                GEOFFREY GORER

JW: *Are you a romantic?*
EA: I *am* a romantic. A natural romantic. I believe in the beauty, dignity, and sacred primacy of the passion that a healthy man feels, instantly, at first sight of a beautiful girl. True to my belief, therefore, I fall desperately in love about ten to fifteen times a

week. Not that I'm greedy; I don't want them all. I just want all the ones I want. If only in my dreams. Naturally I don't discuss this at any great length with my wife. I don't have to; she knows me. A good marriage is one that can survive the ninety-day euphoria of romantic love.

JW: *Are Europeans better at love than Americans?*

EA: We Americans *are* Europeans, at least by heritage. The only significant difference that I'm aware of is the lingering pall of Puritanism, which attempted to deny the power and beauty of sexual love. We have finally escaped that, most of us. But now we find ourselves threatened by a new form of Puritanism called feminism, which attempts to stamp out sex by denying the fundamental and radical differences between men and women. But it is precisely the differences between male and female which create the tension and the delight. If the feminists had their way, the violent pleasures of sexual engagement would be reduced to a kind of mild digital diddling between two, three, or more caponized androgynes clustered on a velveteen water bed. With music by . . . the New Age Neuters?

JW: *What are the essential differences between men and women?*

EA: The essential differences between men and women are biological. Obviously. Not cultural but biological. It is natural, normal, and instinctive for any healthy man to desire many women. It is natural and instinctive for any normal woman to desire a permanent relationship with one man. Why? Because the woman's basic biological function is motherhood; what she wants and needs from a man is reliable protection and support. While any man, if free to do so, would easily impregnate a hundred nubile young females a year—and be happy to get the work. Thus a built-in conflict between the sexes, for which the institution of marriage is the traditional compromise.

JW: *Is the institution of marriage bankrupt?*

EA: No, not marriage—it is our techno-industrial-urbanized society which is bankrupt. When this lunatic asylum called modern civilization collapses, which it will within a century—I'm an optimist—followed by the kind of hunting-and-gathering pastoral life for which human nature is adapted, then the relations between men and women will return to a natural and wholesome basis: man as father, hunter, and warrior; woman as mother, basic provider, keeper of the hearth.

JW: *Can passion survive marriage?*

EA: Passion, sexual passion, may lead to marriage, but cannot sustain marriage. The purpose of marriage is the raising of children, for which patience, not passion, is the necessary foundation.

JW: *What do you think of books like* Women Who Love Too Much?

EA: Harmless placebos for a hypochondriac society.

JW: *Are portrayals of love on TV and in movies accurate?*

EA: Romantic love as depicted on TV and in the movies is derived from courtly love, which was a European invention of the late Middle Ages. Like music, science, philosophy, art, and literature, romantic love has become a traditional component of what we call Western culture. It is based on a way of life blessed with leisure and freedom. It is an aristocratic privilege which our rough approximate democracy strives to make available to all young men and women. I believe in it, I'm in favor of doing all in our power to preserve it, and I think we will succeed. Romantic love will survive the collapse of industrial society, for the same reason that sexual passion will survive—because the two are in essence the same. It is the slavery of agriculture and industrialism which threatens and degrades both.

JW: *What do you think of computer dating?*

EA: Let the computers fuck themselves.

JW: *What do women want?*

EA: That's a dumb question: only a fraud like Freud could make a problem out of an opportunity.

The late EDWARD ABBEY was the author of *The Monkey Wrench Gang, One Life at a Time, Please*, and *The Fool's Progress*.

❧ WOMEN ❧

God created man and, finding him not sufficiently alone, gave him a companion to make him feel his solitude more keenly. PAUL VALÉRY

God made man, and then said I can do better than that and made woman. ADELA ROGERS ST. JOHN

Woman is a constipated biped with a backache.
J. P. GREENHILL

A woman is a creature that's always shopping.
OVID

Women are of two sorts. Some of them are wiser, better learned, discreeter, and more constant than a number of men. But another and a worse sort of them . . . are fond, foolish, wanton, flibbergibs, tatlers, triflers, wavering, witless, without council, feeble, careless, rash, proud, dainty, nice, talebearers, eavesdroppers, rumor-raisers, evil-tongued, worse-minded, and in every way doltified with the dregs of the Devil's dunghill.
BISHOP JOHN AYLMER

Women are an alien race of pagans set down among us. Every seduction is a conversion.
JOHN UPDIKE

Woman: the most beautiful and admirable of fucking machines.
EDMOND AND JULES DE GONCOURT

Heav'n has no rage like love to hatred turn'd,
Nor hell a fury like a woman scorn'd.
                                                        WILLIAM CONGREVE

If a woman hasn't got a tiny streak of a harlot in
her, she's a dry stick as a rule.   D. H. LAWRENCE

The most interesting women characters in a picture are whores, and every man in love is a sex
pervert at heart.   BILLY WILDER

The chaste woman who teases is worse than a
streetwalker.   JAMES G. HUNEKER

Girls who put out are tramps. Girls who don't are
ladies. This is, however, a rather archaic use of the
word. Should one of you boys happen upon a girl
who doesn't put out, do not jump to the conclusion that you have found a lady. What you have
probably found is a lesbian.   FRAN LEBOWITZ

Aren't women prudes if they don't and prostitutes
if they do?   KATE MILLETT

I derive no pleasure from talking with a young
woman simply because she has regular features.
                                                        THOREAU

I have but *nothing* to say to young girls. They're
fine to look at, in the way I would look at a case
filled with Shang dynasty glazes, but expecting to

carry on a conversation with the average teen-aged young lady is akin to reading Voltaire to a cage filled with chimpanzees. I'm certain they would feel the same alienation for me. I can live with that knowledge.   HARLAN ELLISON

I have heard a well-built woman compared in her motion to a ship under sail, yet I would advise no wise man to be her owner if her freight be nothing but what she carries between wind and water.
FRANCIS OSBORNE (advising his son not to marry a beautiful but poor woman)

I should favor anything that would increase the present enormous authority of women and their creative action in their own homes. The average woman . . . is a despot; the average man is a serf.
G. K. CHESTERTON

A woman in love will do almost anything for a man, except give up the desire to improve him.
NATHANIEL BRANDEN

With women, I've got a long bamboo pole with a leather loop on the end of it. I slip the loop around their necks so they can't get away or come too close. Like catching snakes.
MARLON BRANDO

They're asking women to do impossible things. I don't believe women can carry a pack, live in a foxhole, or go a week without a bath.
GENERAL WILLIAM WESTMORELAND

I do not believe in using women in combat, because females are too fierce.   MARGARET MEADE

God, why didn't you make Woman first—when you were *fresh*?   YVES MONTAND in *On a Clear Day You Can See Forever* (screenplay by Alan Jay Lerner)

What do you think: women—a mistake? OR DID HE DO IT TO US ON PURPOSE?
JACK NICHOLSON in *The Witches of Eastwick* (screenplay by Michael Cristofer, from the novel by John Updike)

There is no such thing as an altogether ugly woman—nor altogether beautiful.   MONTAIGNE

Why must women torment me so?
THEODORE DREISER

The great trick with a woman is to get rid of her while she thinks she's rid of you.
SOREN KIERKEGAARD

Being a woman is a terribly difficult trade, since it consists principally of dealing with men.
JOSEPH CONRAD

Women and people of low birth are very hard to deal with. If you are friendly with them, they get out of hand, and if you keep your distance, they resent it.   CONFUCIUS

She is unable to dream, think or love. In a woman, poetry never comes naturally, but always as the result of education. Only the woman of the world *is* a woman; the rest are simply females.
EDMOND AND JULES DE GONCOURT

A beautiful woman who gives pleasure to men serves only to frighten the fish when she jumps in the water. KWANG TSE

The evidence indicates that woman is, on the whole, biologically superior to man. ASHLEY MONTAGU

A male acquaintance once asked Mrs. Patrick Campbell why women seem to have no sense of humor. "God did it on purpose," she replied, "so that we may love you men instead of laughing at you."

The female of the species is more deadly than the male. RUDYARD KIPLING

Women are like dogs really. They love like dogs, a little insistently. And they like to fetch and carry and come back wistfully after hard words, and learn rather easily to carry a basket.
MARY ROBERTS RINEHART

The greater part of what women write about women is mere sycophancy to man.
MADAME DE STAËL

As any psychologist will tell you, the worst thing
you can possibly do to a woman is to deprive her
of a grievance.   BEVERLY NICHOLS

There is something still more to be dreaded than a
Jesuit and that is a Jesuitess.   EUGENE SUE

A man admires a woman not for what she says,
but for what she listens to.
          GEORGE JEAN NATHAN

Woman serves as a looking glass possessing the
magic powers of reflecting the figure of man at
twice its natural size.   VIRGINIA WOOLF

In nine cases out of ten, a woman had better show
more affection than she feels.   JANE AUSTEN

Certain women should be struck regularly, like
gongs.   NOEL COWARD

Intimacies between women often go backwards,
beginning in revelations and ending in small talk
without loss of esteem.   ELIZABETH BOWEN

It is hard, if not impossible, to snub a beautiful
woman—they remain beautiful and the snub recoils.
          WINSTON CHURCHILL

Beautiful women must think about their beauty as
capitalists think about their investments or politicians about their majorities; it is all they have to
insure their places in the world.
          CYRIL CONNOLLY

The last thing a woman will consent to discover in
a man whom she loves, or on whom she simply
depends, is want of courage.   JOSEPH CONRAD

The woman who is really kind to dogs is always
one who has failed to inspire sympathy in men.
MAX BEERBOHM

Women fail to understand how much men hate
them.   GERMAINE GREER

A woman will sometimes forgive the man who
tries to seduce her, but never the man who misses
an opportunity when offered.   TALLYERAND

A woman can forgive a man the harm he does her;
but she can never forgive him for the sacrifices he
makes on her account.   W. SOMERSET MAUGHAM

Men want a woman whom they can turn on and
off like a light switch.   IAN FLEMING

I like clean ladies and nice ladies.
LAWRENCE WELK

Blondes have the hottest kisses. Red-heads are
fair-to-middling torrid, and brunettes are the
frigidest of all. It's something to do with hormones, no doubt.   RONALD REAGAN

A woman may have a witty tongue or a stinging
pen but she will never laugh at her own individual
shortcomings.   IRVIN S. COBB

Women see through each other, but they rarely look into themselves. THEODOR REIK

It is strange how little sharpsightedness women possess; they only notice whether they please, then whether they arouse pity, and finally, whether you look for compassion from them. That is all; come to think of it, it may even be enough, generally speaking. FRANK KAFKA

We throw the whole drudgery of creation on one sex, and then imply that no female of any delicacy would initiate any effort in that direction. GEORGE BERNARD SHAW

To babble is to make a feminine noise somewhat resembling the sound of a brook, but with less meaning. OLIVER HERFORD

Nothing so stirs a man's conscience or excites his curiosity as a woman's silence. THOMAS HARDY

We have drugs to make women speak, but none to keep them silent. ANATOLE FRANCE

A man running after a hat is not half so ridiculous as a man running after a woman. G. K. CHESTERTON

A beautiful woman seductively dressed will never catch cold no matter how low cut her gown. NIETZSCHE

Contrary to popular belief, English women do not wear tweed nightgowns.   HERMIONE GINGOLD

Women dress alike all over the world: they dress to be annoying to other women.
ELSA SCHIAPARELLI

A witch and a bitch always dress up for each other, because otherwise the witch would upstage the bitch, or the bitch would upstage the witch, and the result would be havoc.
TENNESSEE WILLIAMS

Most women dress as if they had been a mouse in a previous incarnation, or hope to be one in the next.   EDITH SITWELL

In mixed company women practice a kind of visual shorthand that they later decode in detail in other women's company.   MALCOLM DE CHAZAL

Never try to outsmart a woman, unless you are another woman.   WILLIAM LYON PHELPS

After a woman reaches fifty, she is usually called upon to deny her weight as well as her age.
ED HOWE

There are three intolerable things in life—cold coffee, lukewarm champagne, and overexcited women.   ORSON WELLES

I will not say that women have no character—they have a different one every day. HEINRICH HEINE

The first duty of a woman is to be pretty, the second is to be well-groomed, and the third is never to contradict. W. SOMERSET MAUGHAM

A woman uses her intelligence to find reasons to support her intuition. G. K. CHESTERTON

There is always something a woman will prefer to the truth. SAMUEL JOHNSON

Women have a hard enough time in this world: telling them the truth would be too cruel.
H. L. MENCKEN

Women are one of the Almighty's enigmas to prove to men that He knows more than they do.
ELLEN GLASGOW

No is no negative in a woman's mouth.
SIR PHILIP SIDNEY

All sensible men are of the same opinion about women, and no sensible man ever says what that opinion is. SAMUEL BUTLER

The penalty for getting the woman you want is that you must keep her.
LIONEL STRACHEY

For me a woman who wears no perfume has no future. PAUL VALÉRY

There are no woman composers, never have been and possibly never will be.

SIR THOMAS BEECHAM

There are not and never have been any great women poker players.

HEYWOOD BROUN

How womanly it is to ask the unaswerable at the moment impossible.

CHRISTOPHER MORLEY

The man who asks a woman what she wants deserves all that's coming to him.

ALEC WAUGH

A woman will buy anything she thinks the store is losing money on.

KIN HUBBARD

A woman does not spend all her time in buying things; she spends part of it in taking them back.

EDGAR WATSON HOWE

There are no social differences—till women come in.

H. G. WELLS

Somewhere in the shadow cast by every famous man is a feminine victim.

JULES RENARD

If I were a girl, I'd despair; the supply of good women far exceeds that of the men who deserve them.

ROBERT GRAVES

Some women like to sit down with trouble as if it were knitting.

ELLEN GLASGOW

Women do not like timid men. Cats do not like prudent mice. H. L. MENCKEN

A woman may be as wicked as she likes, but if she isn't pretty it won't do her much good.
W. SOMERSET MAUGHAM

It is the plain women who know about love; the beautiful women are too busy being fascinating.
KATHARINE HEPBURN

To understand one woman is not necessarily to understand any other woman.
JOHN STUART MILL

For a man to pretend to understand women is bad manners; for him really to understand them is bad morals. HENRY JAMES

No matter how long he lives, no man ever becomes as wise as the average woman of forty-eight.
H. L. MENCKEN

Time and trouble will tame an advanced young woman, but an advanced old woman is uncontrollable by any earthly force. DOROTHY L. SAYERS

The cleverest woman on earth is the biggest fool on earth with a man. DOROTHY PARKER

Fifty percent of the world are women, yet they always seem a novelty. CHRISTOPHER MORLEY

It's the nature of women not to love when we love
them, and to love when we love them not.
CERVANTES

Misogynist: a man who hates women as much as
women hate one another. H. L. MENCKEN

Only a jackass ever talks over his affairs with a
woman, whether she be his sweetheart, wife, or
sister, or mother. H. L. MENCKEN

There is no sincerity like a woman telling a lie.
CECIL PARKER in *Indiscreet*
(screenplay by Norman Krasna)

Now what I love in women is, they won't
Or can't do otherwise than lie, but do it
So well, the very truth seems falsehood to it.
LORD BYRON

A woman's place is in the wrong.
JAMES THURBER

Women never reason, and therefore they are (com-
paratively) seldom wrong. WILLIAM HAZLITT

Women would rather be right than reasonable.
OGDEN NASH

If women didn't exist all the money in the world would have no meaning.   ARISTOTLE ONASSIS

From birth to age eighteen a girl needs good parents, from eighteen to thirty-five she needs good looks, from thirty-five to fifty-five she needs a good personality. From fifty-five on, she needs good cash.   SOPHIE TUCKER

Women are most fascinating between the age of thirty-five and forty after they have won a few races and know how to pace themselves. Since few ever pass forty, maximum fascination can continue indefinitely.   CHRISTIAN DIOR

A woman is as old as she looks before breakfast.   ED HOWE

Those who run around with women don't walk tightropes. They find it hard enough to crawl on the ground.   ISAAC BASHEVIS SINGER

No woman is worth the loss of a night's sleep.   SIR THOMAS BEECHAM

With women you don't have to talk your head off. You just say a word and let them fill in from there.   SATCHEL PAIGE

Life is not long enough for a coquette to play all her tricks.   JOSEPH ADDISON

The entire being of a woman is a secret which should be kept.   ISAK DINESEN

Housekeeping in common is for women the acid
test. ANDRÉ MAUROIS

There is no fury like a woman searching for a new
lover. CYRIL CONNOLLY

There are only three things to be done with a
woman. You can love her, suffer for her, or turn
her into literature. LAWRENCE DURRELL

Is it too much to ask that women be spared the
daily struggle for superhuman beauty in order to
offer it to the caresses of a subhumanly ugly mate?
GERMAINE GREER

Let men do their duty and the women will be
such wonders; the female lives from the light of
the male: see a male's female dependents, you
know the man. WILLIAM BLAKE

A lady's imagination is very rapid; it jumps from
admiration to love, from love to matrimony in a
moment. JANE AUSTEN

Women can always be caught; that's the first rule
of the game. OVID

In all the woes that curse our race
There is a lady in the case. W. S. GILBERT

Women's hearts are like old china, none the worse
for a break or two. W. SOMERSET MAUGHAM

Women are silver dishes into which we put golden
apples. GOETHE

Sphinxes without secrets.   OSCAR WILDE

Women are like dreams—they are never the way
you would like to have them.
                    LUIGI PIRANDELLO

A woman springs a sudden reproach on you which
provokes a hot retort—and then she will presently
ask you to apologize.   MARK TWAIN

A woman's desire for revenge outlasts all her other
emotions.   CYRIL CONNOLLY

For years they have been using the role of "sex
object" as a cover while they spied out the land.
                    ANATOLE BROYARD

No woman ever hates a man for being in love
with her; but many a woman hates a man for
being her friend.   ALEXANDER POPE

On one issue at least, men and women agree: they
both distrust women.   H. L. MENCKEN

In point of morals, the average woman is, even for
business, too crooked.   STEPHEN LEACOCK

Why can't a woman be more like a man?
                    ALAN J. LERNER

I'm not denyin' the woman are foolish: God Almighty made 'em to match the men.
                    GEORGE ELIOT

American women are fools because they try to be everything to everybody.   VIVA

I love being a woman. You can cry. You get to wear pants now. If you're on a boat and it's going to sink, you get to go on the rescue boat first. You get to wear cute clothes. It must be a great thing, or so many men wouldn't be wanting to do it.
                                    GILDA RADNER

Being a woman is of special interest only to aspiring male transsexuals. To actual women it is merely a good excuse not to play football.
                                    FRAN LEBOWITZ

Who am I supposed to be attracted to in this silly culture? That excited woman waxing a shiny surface? No. That woman with capped teeth and terrifying hairdo? No. Try *Showtime*. That slim, shirtless woman with puckered lips, circling a gawking boy? No.   IAN SHOALES

I know no more about women today than when I was in high school.   DAVID LETTERMAN

We have no faith in ourselves. I have never met a woman who, deep down in her core, really believes she has great legs. And if she suspects that she *might* have great legs, then she's convinced that she has a shrill voice and no neck.
                                    CYNTHIA HEIMEL

When the candles are out, all women are fair.

PLUTARCH

For a man there are three certainties in life: death, taxes, and women. It is often difficult to say which is the worst.　　DR. ALBERT ELLIS

The game women play is men.　　ADAM SMITH

Women have two weapons—cosmetics and tears.

NAPOLEON I

There's a lot of difference between a dog and a woman. When you come home at night, a dog don't care where you been.　　LEWIS GRIZZARD

Women are always attracted to power. I do not think there could ever be a conqueror so bloody that most women would not willingly lie with him in the hope of bearing a son who would be every bit as ferocious as the father.　　GORE VIDAL

I wish Adam had died with all his ribs in his body.

BOUCICAULT

When I have one foot in the grave I will tell the truth about women. I shall tell it, jump into my coffin, pull the lid over me and say, "Do what you like now."　　TOLSTOY

These impossible women! How they do get around us! The poet was right: can't live with them, or without them.　　ARISTOPHANES

❧ WHAT DO WOMEN WANT? ❧

The great question that has never been answered and which I have not yet been able to answer, despite my thirty years of research into the feminine soul, is: *What does woman want?*

SIGMUND FREUD

What this woman wants, with all due respect to S. Freud, is for men to stop asking that question and to realize that women are human beings, not some alien species. They want the same things men want.

DIANE WHITE

Different things mostly. What's more, they are kind enough to tell you.   NORMAN COUSINS

Tenderness, sensitivity, caring and security.

LIZ SMITH

I haven't the slightest idea.   TAD SZULC

Attention.   IAN SHOALES

Implicit obedience.   HORACE RUMPOLE

Men.   MALCOLM FORBES

Women want men, careers, money, children, friends, luxury, comfort, independence, freedom, respect, love and a three-dollar pantyhose that won't run.

PHYLLIS DILLER

Never before in history have women known *less* about what they want. The Women's Revolution has created utter chaos and confusion re definition of biological and social roles. The death rate among women will exceed that of men, eventually, from stress. If the *Titanic* sank today, the lifeboats would be full of men because the women and children couldn't run as fast or push as hard. A helluva progress!   EDA LE SHAN

Women want a family life that glitters and is stable. They don't want some lump spouse watching ice hockey in the late hours of his eighteenth beer. They want a family that is so much fun and is so smart that they look forward to Thanksgiving rather than regarding it with a shudder. That's the glitter part. The stable part is, obviously, they don't to be one bead on a long necklace of wives. They want, just like men, fun, love, fame, money and power. And equal pay for equal work.   CAROLYN SEE

Money, power, love, sex (until they get married), adulation, children, and control. Of these, children cause the most trouble. Women also want equal rights and equal pay for equal work, and I agree with them 100%. Though on some days it is hard to figure how a species that controls 97% of the money and *all* the pussy can be downtrodden.
                                         LARRY L. KING

The seemingly impossible: that men treat them with the respect and fairmindedness with which they treat most men.   JOYCE CAROL OATES

Charge cards.   W. P. KINSELLA

Exactly what men want: love, money, excitement, pleasure, happiness, fulfilling work—and sometimes a child who will say, "I love you."
                                        JOYCE BROTHERS

I'd like to own Texas and lease Colorado.
                                        RITA MAE BROWN

What do women want? God, this is awful hard. Various women of course want various things. I think what they really want underneath everything is self-respect. Self-respect. It's a lot easier in our world for a man to achieve self-respect than for a woman. A thing my wife and I are fond of kicking around as a joke is, "I'm just a housewife." You might hear this at a middle class dinner table when talking about a serious subject. You turn to a woman and you say, "What do you think about it?" and she says, "Oh, I'm just a housewife?" No man would say that. No man would say, "I'm just an accountant." He'd have an opinion and he'd utter it. It's harder for a woman to gain self-respect than for a man, and I think this is really what they want more than anything else, and I think that's what the women's movement is largely about.   PAUL FUSSELL

Like everything else, it depends on the individual. It's a subdivision of what do people want. They want to be themselves, they want to reach their own potential. Some of them want men, some of them want women, some of them want neither, some of them want a pet turtle. The bottom line is self-expression.   PAUL KRASSNER

Freedom from pain, security, creature comforts, and an end to loneliness. When you get down to the basics, it's still the same old story, a fight for love and glory . . .   ALICE KAHN

Women are wonderful and complete and the source of beauty and creativity and love. But they are brought up to believe they are inadequate and insufficient and that to be complete and fulfilled they need a ·man. This erroneous notion leads them to seek fulfillment outside themselves, which in turn reinforces their belief in their inadequacy and keeps them in a vicious circle of continually seeking answers outside themselves rather than in discovering at their core that they are already fine and magnificent and complete and that if they lived from their centers all would work out and they could again become the source of creation in the world.   ARI KIEV

They want to stay forever JUNG, and they want a man who is both REICH and HORN(E)Y. Hope you don't regard these effusions as too RANK.
                                              HARRY ZOHN

Any idiot would know women's needs are simple. All we want is your basic millionaire/brain surgeon/ criminal lawyer/great dancer who pilots his own Lear Jet and owns oceanfront property. On the other hand, things being what they are today, most of us will settle for a guy who holds down a steady job and isn't carrying an infectious disease.

LINDA SUNSHINE

> What do women want? A guy they can't drive crazy. There aren't many around. But they try. They can't help it, it's their nature.
>
> ORSON BEAN

None of your business.   URSULA K. LE GUIN

ABOUT THE AUTHOR

Jon Winokur, the author of *The Portable Curmudgeon* and *Zen to Go,* lives in Pacific Palisades, California. Alone.